China
Girl

China Girl

SHORT STORIES

Ho Lin

A *Caveat Lector* Book

REGENT PRESS
Berkeley, California

[paperback]
ISBN 13: 978-1-58790-384-7
ISBN 10: 1-58790-384-9

[hardback]
ISBN 13: 978-1-58790-403-5
ISBN 10: 1-58790-403-9

[e-book]
ISBN 13: 978-1-58790-385-4
ISBN 10: 1-58790-385-7

Library of Congress Control Number: 2017931725

Cover designed by Sean Miner

Author photo by Andrew Steinmetz

Ho Lin: www.holinauthor.com

Caveat Lector: www.caveat-lector.org

Manufactured in the U.S.A.
REGENT PRESS
Berkeley, California
www.regentpress.net

Dedicated to the memory of my mother,
Alice P. Lin

CONTENTS

China Girl

S HE LIKES THIS AMERICAN, THIS MAN WITH NO
job and nothing past a first name. Hair shaggy and
strong, knife-edge wrinkles about his eyes, he booms:
Hang on!

He treats her to rides in his chauffeured sedan. Having a
chauffeur is not unusual in Beijing—anyone who calls himself *Big Brother* seems to have one—but this American grins
like a child, intoxicated by the novelty of it. She can only
imagine what favors he surrenders for the privilege. Debts
measured in restaurant tabs, shapely bottles of Yanjing beer
clanging in toasts, hordes of red intoxicated faces.

The American's driver is Chinese. He greets her with
smiling crooked teeth. Many times before she has seen his
kind: the ingratiating *yes,* the accommodating *okay.* She
ponders whether he screams at his children, or orders his
wife to assume kinky sexual positions.

The December roads are slab-like. The driver, over-
compensating as usual, has the heat on full blow, and yet
she clings to the American, wanting to get beneath that
bulbous ski jacket, lay hands on his sweaty shirt. With
easy laughter, he tickles her, outmaneuvers her. *Where to
tonight?* he whispers. *Tell me. So what if we're in China? We*

can go anywhere. She is struck by his voice, the confidence of it, tough and ignorant and unassailable.

She sees the construction truck, the fat steel pipes jutting from the back of it, even before the Audi skids on a particularly crafty scrap of ice. The driver hits the brakes, which only accelerates the uncontrolled spin. The pipes are now rushing towards them, towards the region of windshield before the American's face.

He sees them now too, and all he shouts is: *Hang on!* As if he is spitting on his hands and getting straight to work.

Posing nude, stretched out on her side, she chews gum and reads a comic. The photographer from Lucky Life Studios is a roundish man with an apologetically wrinkled shirt, and his voice never rises above a murmur. He asks simple questions: *What do you think about this arm, just so? This leg further out, maybe?* He illustrates with a dainty gesture, and for a languorous moment, there is no difference between him and her.

She nods *yes* and *no* accordingly, and all the while chews hard. So disgusting, my anxiety, this newfound prudishness, she thinks. She has snorted at commercials for breast-enlarging creams, contemplated cosmetic ads of Joan Chen and her blood-berry lips, and paused to admire the proportion of her own arms, the circumference of her ankles. But under the lamp's hot sun, she feels misshapen, the little dip of fat around her stomach hanging there, as if gorging on the light.

Red fabric approximating a velvet curtain lounges on the wall behind her—looking closely at it, one can see corpse-like dust. In the corner, a window gouges out territory, and just beyond it, the traffic honks on and on in the gray morning. A mosquito whines at her ear. She turns toward it, wishing to inquire: *How are you feeling today?* The photographer exclaims, for the composition he was planning has vanished, and a more seductive pose has taken its place. He rushes to say: *Wait! That's good, wait!*

The comic book is just beyond camera shot, at her hip, and as she turns the pages they tickle her. A flyer peeks out. *Are you a woman with a tale to tell?* An editor is looking for stories of Chinese women's love lives: office affairs, unwanted pregnancies, runaway girls. Confidentiality assured.

The photographer asks her to raise her head, as if she is regarding a sudden, amorous visitor. *More concentration,* he says, hands before his face, blocking all but his eyes. *A serious look. Hollywood model pose. Very nice.* Unconsciously, he is recreating a pose from youth, a courageous female cadre urging on her comrades with a defiant rise of the chin, forever looking into the unknown distance. The mosquito alights on his arm. With an annoyed slap he crushes it. The blood spreads on his skin like abstract art. Across the comic's open pages, a lone swordsman whirls, his weapon slashing with tornado-like force, the inked waves of his assault threatening to burst out of the page.

She watches her older sister yell at her parents. Her family's tiny, stone-hued apartment is a complete disaster: half-opened paint cans, canvas crumpled in gobs, ribbons of wallpaper like obscenely gigantic toilet rolls. Her sister's boyfriend and his comrade huddle against the wall, army jackets draped about their shoulders, their hands close to their faces as they whisper and laugh, jolly as monks.

You have to pay them! her sister shouts. *They've already bought all this stuff, you have to pay them!*

Are you crazy? Her mother's face is as wide as a tiger's, her mouth bulging, rampaging. *What are you doing, just walking in here and telling us you're going to do this?*

Of course we're doing this! This place is filthy. Unfit for pigs, even! Aren't you embarrassed to have friends visit?

What do you care? You're never at home anyway!

I tell you, he's good! Don't you know Army people can't live on only their salaries these days? They all get side jobs. He's already repainted three apartments!

With a volcanic shift of the throat, the boyfriend hacks mucus into his mouth. He leans over, seized by habit, ready to spit it all out onto the floor, but then holds himself up, barely. A thread of drool falls out, connects his lips to his chest.

When we're ready, we'll renovate the apartment. Her mother theatrically takes her time in folding her arms.

You'll be dead before that happens! Hey! She snaps her fingers at the two army men. *Let's get started. It's no use arguing with her.* She picks up a paint can.

All through this her father has been silent. Now he runs a perplexed hand through what is left of his hair. *Well, it's no big deal. We can spend a little money, can't we?*

But her mother and her sister are now engaged in a tug of war over the can. Both their knuckles go white as they yell at each other: —*Let go!* —*You let go!* —*We're going to do this!* —*No you're not!* —*You pig-headed idiot!* Her father is frantically rummaging in his pockets for his wallet. The boyfriend stares dumbly at the scene.

For no reason at all, she remembers an incident from when she was six. She had accompanied her father to the office where he was supposed to pick up his pay. Already a few dozen co-workers were milling about, impatient in a friendly way: *Hey, should we get breakfast and lunch first, or what?* Behind a creaky wooden desk with a short leg, a woman was brandishing a ruler like a weapon, yelling at them all to stop chattering and line up single-file. Then she sat down and began counting money. The minutes stretched out to half an hour, even more. The room went foggy with the workers' cigarettes, but still the woman sat there, arranging money in tidy piles, one perfect little stack after another, obviously enjoying her power, the table sometimes tipping onto the short leg when she laid a bill down.

She was too young to be angry, but several times she pulled at her father's sleeve: *Dad, should I go up there and ask her why she's taking so long?* Her father shook his head. *We have to be patient,* he said soothingly. *There's nothing we can do.*

She walks up to her sister and mother and with a deft flick of the wrist, tips the can. Paint spills out in an abbreviated flood. Most of it lands on her sister's lap, some finds her mother's coarse stockings. Before either of them can even shriek in surprise, she is out of the apartment, trotting down the steps, past the open-mouthed neighbors who have gathered to eavesdrop.

She calls a Holiday Inn in America. Ordinarily dialing toll-free numbers from a public phone is an impossibility, but one of her friends—she forgets who now—gave her the code. At a rickety wooden stand on Renmin Road, phones lined up like toys on the sill, clutching the dirtied white receiver to her ear and mouth, she endures two housewives on both sides of her having identical conversations: *home* and *dinner* and *relatives* and *Where are you?*

This time a pleasant man answers. She savors the long-distance lag in their conversation, the extra seconds she must take to speak: *Hello! I would like to make a reservation.*

Of course, he says. Professional, to the point, he requests

location and time, and she gives it to him. Today she is
Ms. Wang; last week she was Ms. Lee, and the week before
that Ms. Zhang. Today it is Los Angeles, last week it was
Boston, the week before that, Las Vegas. Always one week
ahead for the reservation—it is too depressing to consider
lengths of time any further along than that.

Thank you, Ms. Wang, the helpful reservation agent
says. *Have yourself a wonderful day.*

Thank you, she says. She almost forgets to add *You have
a nice day too,* but this time she remembers. Alas, the man
has already hung up. American politeness is a tricky thing
to negotiate.

A bus hacks diesel smoke at her. Bicycle bells ring like
nagging mothers. She looks down at her sandals, her bare
feet: dirt already stuck under her toenails. Nearby a food
cart serves fried dough, the single waffle-sized block of coal
in its oven smoldering so intensely her eyes water. One evening she will sail into the Holiday Inn, be it New York or
Chicago or San Francisco, announce her identity, and lie
flat on her room's rich, open, carpeted floor all night.

She enjoys visiting her musician friends. Beijingers by
birth, they are both guitarists—Does anyone truly want to
play bass, or are all bassists forced to their instruments by
the tyrannical guitar virtuosos? she wonders—and make
their home in a Dongzhimen apartment with the color and
texture of a well-used ash tray. She snuggles up with a wet
bottle of beer and gazes at the steam-cracked walls as they
noodle about. The agenda always includes an exact cover
of "Hotel California," the version from *Hell Freezes Over.*

You ever write your own songs? she asks.

Of course, the handsome one snaps. Here, now, he is
formidable, but she saw him play once at the Star Shower

café during an open mike, and he went all tight and robotic as he improvised a blues tune. She still remembers how he slumped, his stringy hair hiding his face, as the bar patrons good-naturedly applauded his timidity, and how endearing it was.

The handsome one is the leader, the singer, but the not-so-handsome one is the better player. Bobbing his head up and down, his glasses prancing on the bridge of his nose, he coaxes machine-gun rhythms from his acoustic. Before she can even say *Nirvana,* the handsome one begins singing, in English. She cannot make out the lyrics, but at the beginning of every line, he moans *Kurt Cobain ... Kurt Cobain ...*

She doesn't ask about the song after they have finished, for she knows that the handsome one considers songs a divine gift, beyond the bounds of explanation. He pops in a VCD of Michael Jackson videos, pre-*Thriller* days. *His early songs are fresher,* the not-so-handsome one says in a most earnest tone. *Can't stop till you get enough,* Michael sings over and over, and the handsome one passes his cigarette among the three of them.

I hear that Americans treat their dogs well, the handsome one murmurs. His face is fiery from beer. *Clean them all the time, care for them like children, build houses for them—shit, they even build tombs for them!* Swept up with the thought of it, he flops back onto his squeaky board-like bed. *Fuck, I wish I was an American dog!*

She passes her cigarette to him and he takes it with long, feminine fingers. She is jealous of those fingers. He puffs distractedly, and after a while his eyes lock on her, but she is watching the video. The sunset throws orange into the cramped room, Michael sings and dances in place, and even though she now knows he is staring at her, she continues to watch the video. She is surprised to discover she is completely content.

She works at a local dance club twice a week. *May Lee!* the DJ screams as she trots out of the shadows and the spotlight finds her. Her job is simple. She must climb the twisty stairs until she is on the smallish platform one story above the floor. Once there, she gyrates, pulses, thrusts. *Give it up for May Lee!* Her name is not May Lee, it is merely a pseudonym. Spotlights now dance like fireflies. The thud of relentless basslines shakes the platform beneath her. On the ground, a foreigner is shouting at her. She guesses American, as he lacks that European bearing, that aura of aloofness. *May!* he chants. *May May May May May!*

She smiles at him. Three weeks she has worked at this club, and she is still amazed at how rarely people smile. One could almost believe them to be comatose if not for their moving bodies, their jerky attempts at spontaneity. A nation of stone-faced ballroom dancers, she concludes sadly—sure you can learn the foxtrot and the waltz like you memorize poems, but what does that get you?

Above everyone, a miniature spaceship glides on a track nailed to the ceiling, soaring with the *Star Wars* overture. Bomb doors open and confetti scatters everywhere. Below, the American hops in place, snapping hungrily at the floating bits of paper. *May May May May May!*

She tosses a smirk and a wink his way. Yes, there is a point to this black tank-top, these slinky black stockings, this petal-like mini-skirt she must wear. Loose cigarette smoke almost forces a sneeze out of her—*No, no sneezing, it's not sexy.* The American is at the bottom of the stairs, making eyes at her, blocking any means of escape but not quite ready to sweep in and claim the prize. *May May May May May!*

Two Chinese men with shirts unbuttoned to mid-chest

and shiny slick hair appear at his side. They are dancing, but with every movement they bump him, nudge him away from the stairs, shove him further and further out. She now leans over the platform, fully aware of her part in this war, and blows the American a kiss. The American is still chanting her name, although at this distance the contortions of his mouth seem sickly. The two Chinese men are now firmly between him and her, and there is no mistaking their choreography as anything but a not-so-subtle threat: *Stay away from her, Foreign Devil.* The American lays a hand on one of the Chinese men's shoulders. With a sudden jerk, he is grabbed, wrestled down beneath the rolling spotlights.

She laughs, spins around, three hundred sixty degrees, seven hundred twenty, more, her own hair needling her face. Men must always play the games, and she must always encourage them. And when it is all over, one of them says hello, or no one says hello, and either way will be fine with her.

She hates the David Bowie song. Nothing about the melody or words is particularly galling to her, but *that video!* A woman dressed more like a geisha than anything remotely Chinese! That mousy face, that underfed skinny body! How could anyone think of that as a beautiful Chinese girl?

And yet this German with the two-day beard rubs his cheeks against her bare shoulder and hums: *Uh oh oh ohhhhh ... little China girl.* In response, she blows smoke in his face.

Smoking is good for you, he says. She blinks, considers that statement for a moment, and shrugs it off as completely irrelevant.

Now he is complaining about a new expat community outside Beijing. Two-story homes, manicured lawns, local golf courses. *Doesn't that make you mad?* he growls. *Millions of Chinese living hard lives, and these Americans running riot over everything? Building miniature Americas everywhere they go?*

She wants to answer No. Instead she thinks to herself: *It must be deeply satisfying to travel and live in another country, and be able to make those kinds of statements.*

Later in the shower with him, she urinates—something common for her, she doesn't even think about it. The German yelps and dodges away, as if stung, and water splashes out of the tub. *Jesus!* he shouts. *That's disgusting!*

Why? It all goes to the same place, she replies calmly.

He will not even argue. Within moments, he is drying off, looking himself up and down, as if checking for acid burns. Amused and bemused, she stares at him. Now the words of the David Bowie song are coming to her ... something about *stumbling into town,* then a *sacred cow.* What the hell does it all mean? She bites the insides of her cheeks as she puzzles over this affair, and the German stares at himself in the mirror, hypnotized by his own likeness.

She drags her sixteen-year old cousin to Sanlihe District on a Friday evening. Their parents are busy at home chattering and pouncing over *mahjong,* the evening holds the beautiful heavy calm of mid-spring, and the sodium streetlights glow like trapped moonlight. So she decides: *I want a drink.* And her cousin, so slim and so shy in her modest haircut and her monotone white blouse, must come with her.

The district is active tonight. Men dressed in padded suits sidle up to foreign men: *Massage? Sexy lady. Come and see.* At the outdoor bars, expatriates hang all over chairs, laughing and relating and enjoying their little parcels of territory. She feels her cousin's nervous breaths at the back of her neck. Her cousin is talking about Beijing University—*I'm worried about the college exams*—and her eyes refuse to stay still. To her, every person on the street must be a threat—even the policemen, their caps down over their eyes, positively cowed to be in this foreign ghetto.

Nothing will happen, she reassures her cousin. *It'll be all right.*

Her cousin gives a wan nod. *She's so obedient,* the older woman thinks. *Good little girl.* Nevertheless, she likes her.

She wants to hit the Gold Hut down the alley—sometimes her two guitarists are there, running through Doors tunes, and she has not seen them in a while—but in a concession to her cousin's sensibilities, she leads her into a well-lit beerhouse. The Filipino band inside wears frilly clothes, as if this is a wedding party, and leans hard on friendly keyboards and inoffensive pop songs. She orders a bottle of beer, then another, and her cousin grows red with something other than drunkenness.

D-Do Aunt and Uncle know you come here? she finally stammers.

No. She drains her glass too quickly and beer runs down either side of her chin. A fine example of alcohol etiquette you are setting, she thinks. Restlessly, she strikes up a cigarette.

Now her cousin is shrinking, flinching. Under the smoggy houselights the barrettes in her hair seem especially ludicrous.

Here. She pours a fresh glass for her cousin. *Have one.*

Oh, no—

Come on. Drink up. You going to spend all your time studying? Enjoy yourself!

I can't! She immediately jumps up, begins backing away. *I'll—wait outside. I'm too young. I'll be outside. I'll wait for you. I'm too young.* And with that she flees with a tiptoe sprint.

For a time she stares into the crowd where her cousin disappeared. Bodies bump accidentally, squeeze past each other, twist in avoidance, endless combinations. The waiter sets a fresh candle on the table, and she gazes at its fragile light. You should have had a drink, cousin, she thinks. Don't you know that no one in China is too young?

The guitarists are having a party, and she arrives late. She knows something unusual is happening because she can hear the Cui Jian song from their window, three stories up, through the pounding rain. To them, Cui Jian is a boulder around their necks, a constant reminder, for he is an underground rocker gone famous and they decidedly are not.

She trudges upstairs, trailing soggy echoes, her umbrella bogged down with rain. She hears Mr. Cui bellow:

I've given you my dreams,
given you my freedom,
but you always just laugh
at my having nothing—
When will you go with me?

She knocks at their door several times, but in the din no one responds. With a sigh, she lets herself in. There has been some attempt by the guests to be polite, for shoes are lined up by the door, but past that are cigarette butts like bomb debris, sudsy washes of beer across the concrete floor. The oddest odor is now pricking her nose—beer mixed with marijuana mixed with puke.

Hey! The handsome one is stripped to the waist, and by his side are two women, completely naked. There is something modest in the way they stand, and how their knees knock. Unsteady, a seasick chain, they lean leftwards, then rightwards. *Can you take a picture?* the handsome one slurs. *Hurry, we can't stay like this all night …*

One of the women leans in to whisper something in his ear. The other is fiddling with the tiny hairs on his chest, giving his nipple a mischievous tug. He laughs, ticklish, and it is at this moment that she takes the picture.

The not-so-handsome one is bent over the toilet. At first she presumes he is throwing up, but then he rises, and it is clear that he is alert, calm. A glass syringe is in his hand.

What are you doing? she asks.

Experimenting, he says. No, he isn't normal; his eyes are doll-like. The whites of them quaver like the almond gelatin she had at dinner. The liquid in the syringe is yellow, with tiny dark bits scattered throughout.

What is—she begins, but the not-so-handsome one stumbles past her. She turns and a foreigner, apparently the lone foreigner at the party, introduces himself. Fully clothed, dark and clean, he reminds her of Antonio Banderas, but his English is perfect. Quickly, the conversation develops: *You are a teacher? No, just for the year, then back to Seattle.*

And then he says: *I'm the party man.*

What do you mean?

I, um, organized this.

The handsome one chases one of the naked girls past them. She pounds the floor hard with her bare feet, fleeing into the bathroom, the door slamming behind her with a furious *eek.* He delays his pursuit just long enough to grin at Antonio, then throws himself against the door. For a moment she fears it will splinter, but then it bangs open, recoils back into the handsome one's face. He laughs despite the pain, enters the bathroom, slams the door shut again. She hears the girl scream—pain or ecstasy, it is impossible to tell—and very slowly, she rests her hands on her cheeks, close to her ears.

You okay? Antonio asks. *You want?* He offers a marijuana joint. *I also have—*

Help! Someone help!

The not-so-handsome one is convulsing on the floor, the syringe by his side and cracked open. A naked man and woman are on the couch, drawing their scattered clothes around themselves, only their eyes visible above their raised shirts. The foreigner retrieves the syringe, wafts the odor his way, and sniffs. *Oh man,* he groans.

What? she whispers.

Oh man, he says again. *He injected himself with the shit from the toilet ...*

Even as her stomach rebels at the thought of it, she sees that the not-so-handsome one is not moving at all. The foreigner bends over him, stretching his eyelids open, then forces his mouth into a fishlike pout. With an almost phlegmatic movement, he begins mouth-to-mouth resuscitation.

The handsome one is on his knees by her side. *Oh fuck,* he says. *Oh fuck.* His head wobbles this way and that, and even as he rubs his eyes she sees the tears flowing freely. She puts her arms around him, holding him as tight as she has ever held anything, and he trembles with the force of his delirium, his head hard against her shoulder.

This is the third time she has been interviewed by a visa officer. The door to the interview room is slightly ajar, and snatches of conversation from outside infiltrate: an American man is trying to arrange full U.S. citizenship for his Chinese wife.

You should have done this already, she hears someone say. *Why are you even here? Why are you wasting my time? You have to fill this out and have it authorized by the local authorities. It's not my job to do it for you.*

Why do you want to go to America? the visa officer asks.

Her current boyfriend from Austin has coached her on the answer, and she speaks fluently, if not flawlessly—this is intentional, for a smoothly recited answer gives the game away. *In my particular field of my study ... best program ... feel like I can contribute to scholarly studies not only in China, but America as well ... Eetcetera.*

I see you've already been accepted at UT Austin, he says. *Good school.*

This is new to her, this kindness. Her previous interviewer simply scowled, unblinking, as if awaiting any weakness that would manifest itself immediately on her own features. *You want to go to America, you have to prove you have a good reason,* he had said. At the end of the interview, he had shaken his head. *Not good enough,* he said, and that was that.

But now this interviewer is smiling, his breath sweet with coffee, and telling her that her school is good. This is unexpected. She knows that an American smile means nothing, but still she returns it with a shy one of her own, and it is at this moment that she realizes her heart is pounding with excitement. *It's going to work,* she realizes.

And they gave you a scholarship, he continues. *That's great.*

They are very generous, she says modestly. This is good, this modest business.

You have official permission from your government to go?

She produces the paper. Still his smile is big and bold and beautiful. Who first described America that way? Did they know how right they were?

And someone has agreed to be your sponsor?

Yes, she has that paper too. Signed by her boyfriend, who pilfered the company letterhead from his father's cement factory.

Are you working right now?

No, she says. Not entirely true, she is working part-time, but she can't talk about the dance club with a man in a suit.

Still he smiles. But wait, now he shakes his head. Smiling and shaking the head? A conundrum to stump even Buddha.

Your credentials are good, he says. *But—*

No! she nearly bursts out. She has stood on the street all morning, in line with the dozens of others who have come to the U.S. embassy for the very same thing, stamping her feet in the chill, looking down at her shoes for every passerby or local policeman who stared at her, every silent judge of her motives and loyalty.

But she stays quiet. She only half-hears the rest. Something about limits. Quotas. *So many applications. We prefer people who have steady jobs. It means they are earning to support ... difficult to turn away worthy people ...* She is now standing, shaking a hand, or rather, a hand is shaking her. Through the slightly open door, back to the central reception area. Head awhirl, she thinks: *I will get this Austin man to marry me. I could convince him to do it, he loves me just enough. And then it would be all right.*

The American man and his Chinese wife are still arguing with the embassy official, who glares from behind a window, his glasses hanging obscenely low under his eyes. *Who the hell do you think you are?* the American man is shouting. *I'm an American citizen!*

I don't care, the official says, and she is taken aback by the venom in his voice. It is completely unlike the rudeness of the street merchants, their offhand cruelty. This is a tone calculated to hurt, like the brutal twist of a knife even after it has pierced the victim's heart.

The American man is still raging. His wife meets her eyes, and looks down at the floor. Already a Marine guard is at the door, his hand at his sidearm, appraising the situation. He pushes past her with an unnecessary shove, and even as she struggles to regain her balance, even as her momentum takes her out of the room, she laughs once, a near-hysterical giggle. *What am I thinking?* she wonders. *Why would I marry him?*

She is supposed to rendezvous with the handsome guitarist at the front gate of their alma mater. Held up in traffic for an hour—They add ring roads and ring roads, and all it does is breed more drivers, she huffs—she finally gives up and exits the taxi a kilometer away. *Hey, I can't let you out here, I'll get in trouble,* the taxi driver whines, but she thrusts an extra 10 yuan bill at him and stomps off without a word.

Dust kicks up in her eyes. When she graduated two years before, this was a two-lane road, divided cleanly down the center by a line of plump trees. Now, it is a pseudo-highway, six lanes across, gravel and dirt and the diesel gas that leaves that scratchy stickiness in your throat. She fumbles for tissues, realizes she neglected to take any in her rush out the door. She is forced to buy a roll of toilet paper from a local stand. She rubs her eyes with it, and it feels as if they are being scratched with stones. Half-blinded, she stumbles past unfamiliar geographic landmarks. The Dunkin Donuts over there now a Kenny Rogers Rotisserie Chicken. The alley behind the university, once so foul and cluttered with grimy restaurants and construction rubble, now home to bootleg DVD stores and clear-paneled windows. Detesting this hotter-than-usual August and the dampness in her armpits, she walks on.

Now she is half an hour late, and as she nears the gates, she debates what she should say. Harried: *Really sorry I'm late, this damn traffic.* Or playful: *Rock stars are never on time—you expect me to be?* Or just concerned: *Haven't seen you in a while, are you okay?*

Halfway between the university gates and the street, a small crowd has gathered around something. Giving in to the ravenous curiosity that she sometimes hates to see in others, she hurries over, shoves against the sweaty wall, and breaks through just enough to see what they are looking at.

The handsome one is on his side, in a fetal position. His lips are open, and she can see the tips of his cigarette-stained teeth. The white T-shirt at his throat is dyed red, and the stain runs down his side, onto the sizzling concrete. He stares straight ahead, as if taking extra care to pose for a portrait.

Her sight goes blurry as she holds a hand to her head. Conversations ricochet:

—*Just a few minutes ago*—

—*Fight in that bar over there*—

—*They chased him over here*—

—*The two of them ganged up on him, one held him down, the other cut him*—

—*So fast, like a dream*—

At the university gates, the two guards stand sentry,

unmoving, staring straight ahead, their helmets smart on their heads. Mouth yawing open, she wants to yell at them, scream *Do something, you bastards!* But there is still a fragment of reason in her head that mutters: *It is not their concern. It is not their job.*

More and more people are gathering. Already some are edging up to the body, like scavengers probing the prey for signs of life. With a single tortured breath, she shoves past all of them, falls to her knees by his side. She reaches out and closes his eyes. In the sun, his skin is hot to the touch.

The crowd rears up with a thrilled surge of whispers: *Who is this young woman? Maybe the fight was over her. Why is she still here? The police will give her a hard time.* She disregards it all and stares at his smooth face, his long hair now wilting, the parted lips that for all the world seem to be asking for a drink of water. *You idiot,* she says silently. *Maybe I really cared about you. You idiot.*

The police arrive an hour and a half later, and find her on her knees next to him, having not moved at all. When they help her to her feet, she looks at them with a spectral smile and murmurs, *Someone had to stay. To watch him.*

She runs away. No, she knows putting it like that is too dramatic, although she likes to imagine she is running away. She is merely on a city bus, a bus she has never taken before, on her way to some unknown destination on the north end of town. The trip seems as lengthy and treacherous as traveling the length of a province, and she appreciates the bus's slug-like pace, the rickety way the doors whip open and never quite close completely.

A day later she will return home, her clothes stained from a night spent out in the open at the Perfection and Brightness Garden—in olden days, it was part of the

Imperial Summer Palace, but it has devolved into desolate ponds, wrecked Roman columns, a few trees clumped together. She will find a spot overlooking the dried-up remains of a lake, drink five and a half bottles of beer in the moonlight, and sprinkle the remaining half-bottle onto the sickly brown grass. Her father will be the first to see her when she shambles in the next afternoon, and after she tells him where she has been, he will look at her sadly, and say: *Your mother will talk to you. I can't say anything. I love you too much to get angry.*

The bus is empty except for the driver and the woman who sits near the doors, selling tickets. They exchange words; in appearance they seem to be locals, but their dialect is unintelligible. Friends from the same remote village, she guesses. The driver laughs heartily, his brawny arms holding the wheel tight as they hit another in an ongoing series of potholes, and yells something back to the ticket woman, something warm and vulgar and confidential. The ticket woman guffaws at the brazenness of his remark, and dismisses him with a wave, but they continue smiling at the rear view mirror, at each other.

Tired, she tries to sleep, but the jolts and bumps of the bus are too erratic. It is hot, perhaps the hottest day of the summer, but the wind rushing through the open windows dries her. She buttons up her shirt and wraps her arms around herself. Outside, cicadas buzz about in stereo, and the thin-necked trees sway in great washes of green. She wishes the bus would continue on unhindered, sailing through this verdant alien countryside, but she knows that in a few weeks the leaves will turn, and fall.

Blood-stained Heroes

I'LL KILL YOU! I'LL KILL YOU! THEY SHOUTED,
he and the other children, and they would chase each
other around the playground, every completion of the
circle birthing another gigantic clump of dust, and as they
grew dizzy and hysterical with laughter they imagined they
were skirting a kingdom of clouds, like the mythical war-
riors of old. A bus sometimes bounced past on the craggy
road with a noisy, uneven *bang-bang-bang*. Back then they
had no television, no black cars with tinted windows. They
had only the dirt that turned to mud on their sweaty arms,
their throats raw with screaming, their imaginations forg-
ing golden blades out of broken twigs.

One hot summer afternoon on the playground his
younger brother was driven mad with the heat, and rained
indiscriminate kicks on his knees, his shins. Suddenly
impatient, fed up with the extreme heat, he shoved, and
his brother went down, head to curb. When his brother
rose again blood dribbled like syrup down the side of his
face. He ran towards home with a theatrical wail: *I'm telling
Dad! He's gonna beat you to death!*

Scared beyond reason, he fled, in an unknown

direction. Years later he would realize it was only a few
kilometers, but back then, it was like escaping to another
land. A food stand reeked of almond gelatin. Someone else
was chopping up fish entrails and flinging the half-corpses
to the ground. He treated them like landmines, hopping
awkwardly over them. Street names and store signs lost
meaning, and were reduced to riots of reds and greens and
whites. Peddlers in wide-brimmed hats stared at him; old
men gestured at him, as if he was a spy newly discovered. He
ran from them all, until he came upon an abandoned yard
and the shade of a tree. Years later it would be demolished
by granite sidewalks, and later still, government-sponsored
shacks for the war veterans would squat there, but back
then he collapsed in the welcoming darkness, already
caught in the transition between the nervous thrill of
flight and the reality of hunger, and as he lay there, the sun
dropped from branch to branch, patient like an engorged
drop of water. A wind blew in so confidently that he could
almost believe it was cool. Cicadas chattered by his ear,
warning of the return home, the inevitable humiliation.
He wanted to keep running, and even as his heart sank and
his vision darkened, he insisted to himself: Trees like this
are everywhere. Every time I need a rest, I will find one.
With every tree, another adventure completed, another
fresh dream launched…

* * *

…and in a lazy arc, he tumbles, fully automatic death
leaping from the guns he clutches in both hands. Too
late. If he had turned an instant sooner … or if he was
younger, back in the days when sharpness of sense was like
a perpetual thirst …

Spent cartridges tinkle on the linoleum. For the last time, he inhales gunpowder, the odor akin to rotten oranges. Shattered kneecap touches cold floor, pain as sudden as car high beams in darkness. Minutes before his suit was pressed, the white of angels, immaculate. Now it is soaked, his blood, others' blood, for the cowards have ambushed him, five young ruffians, immortality seekers, and being who he is, even fat and content, he has already made quick work of the other four. His pistols are clicking, dry, empty. In the brief seconds he is on his knees, he sees the skyline outside his office, the canyons of the city he once called his, the spectrums of neon lights meant to be loved through car windows. Then sense fails, muscles flatten, and he sinks.

The last opponent is obviously the leader. Those designer sunglasses are the giveaway, today's name brands signifying as much as a banner or man-high scroll in the old days. Now the glasses hang lopsided on his face as he falls. They both lay on their sides, febrile like animals in noonday heat, facing each other. He has only enough strength to pull the sunglasses from his face. His opponent, the same. His lips part to say something, but the rigidity of death is upon him, slowing every action, congealing it. His nemesis's eyes are bulging in realization. Perhaps dead already. He can only think what the man wanted to say: *Maybe it shouldn't have happened like this* ... And his head lolls, his gaze drops to the floor, where blood traces the grooves within the tiles, as if a message is written there ...

* * *

...and he knows all eyes are upon him as he presses the wine-dark tip of his brush to the paper. One more stroke and he is done, one final flick, bravado in his nonchalance, but if he is careless with the pressure, if he pauses for even an instant too long, then the strong line will be shattered, and the work of the other strokes, the perfect proportions of the other characters, will be for nothing.

> *Cloud coming out of the city gate*
> *Heavy rain pouring outside the city wall.*

The officials nod approvingly: a Tu Fu poem. Quoting Tu Fu is good. Tu Fu is currently in favor. And it is excellent that he quotes a man who was outspoken, honest, true, banished from the Court to the hinterlands, left with nothing but his poetic fancies under a thatched roof. This is a mark of independence, his decision to quote Tu Fu, for nothing is more suspicious than a man without proclivities.

He knows this is what they are thinking, and hates them for it. They have underestimated him, and always will. Writing these lines is not a show of independence, or a cunning ploy to win favor. It comes straight from within, sculpted with skill and strength and natural, unerring instinct, as necessary as breathing. Joining this court, sitting in the company of these plotters and underminers, with their talk of examinations and merits and the opportunity to bow in the heavenly presence of the Emperor, all of it is sickening. And yet this is the best that this world can offer, this is the greatest honor one can be afforded. He must be of them, like them. Kowtow until his head erupts with bruises. The alternative is conscription, poverty, sickness, death. He must survive. He is sure of that, at least. And even as he completes the stroke, the officials cheer as one for his achievement, and his future locks into place, he thinks of the West Lake, of the early morning mist, the grass glistening with the shine of emeralds, the lonely—or celebratory—cry of a lone bird as it skims the water ...

* * *

... He struggles upstream, the spoiled rags that pass
for his clothes wrapped in a sheet and tied to the end of a
pole. He must hold his nose as he passes the soldiers' bodies.
Motionless arms reach for him, sightless eyes beseech him.
A common sight, these corpses clogging the riverbank like
so much trash, their empty rifles at their sides, decaying,
growing soft and gray together. Once there were fields,
there was farming, but then the foreign soldiers came, the
earth was scorched, his home was cannibalized for wood.
And now he stinks of shit, the soldiers' shit. He wonders
why they couldn't have chosen somewhere simple to relieve
themselves, like a hole in the ground? Deluded, they
insisted on these makeshift shacks, as if privacy matters in
this heat, this desolate land. And at dawn he must shuffle to
these shacks with pails of fetid water dangling heavy from
his arms, douse and splash and wipe and repeat, and all the
while he can hardly breathe, for the urine is palpable, like
mist. Sometimes insurgent snipers station themselves in the
trees atop the far hill and take pot shots at the shack. They
never hit their targets, and this is intentional, for if they
were to kill even one person, the foreign soldiers would
hunt and kill them, and life is always preferable to a small
victory. So it is a delicate balance—they must shoot, for
they are ordered to shoot, but they will never hit a target.
Still, when shots rattle above his head like marauding bees,
the fear chokes him. He must run to the river, to the place
where the bodies are, and he doesn't care, he must wash
himself, so he jumps awkwardly in. The soldiers who are
still alive and lounging nearby in their hard, muddy boots

always laugh, hold their noses, and make jokes in their own language.

But the day has finally come. The soldiers are leaving, and he will accompany them to a land of golden roads and air conditioning and shining white teeth. They load a steamer with supplies and dead comrades, all wrapped in canvas, the bodies more shapely and flexible than the weapons. Now the last unit is boarding, feet in perfect unison, the gangplank bending into a smile under their weight. He rushes to join them, but the sweaty pink sergeant halts him with a hand on his shoulder. They argue, demands and insults traded in their own languages, until finally a translator arrives: *No more room on the ship. We don't have any more room.*

But you're carrying dead people! he yells.

These bodies must go home, the translator insists.

He begins again: *I helped you, I did what no one else … I must …* but the sergeant has lost patience. With a shove, he is slammed into the water, everything he owns soaked. The steamer belches fresh smoke, and begins its journey downriver. Knee-deep in mud, he watches, cursing the mosquitoes, the overgrown weeds, the endless clear sky. *Foreign devils!* he screams. As if in answer, something rumbles from nearby, the fury of an entire thunderstorm contained in a single soaring sound. He instinctively ducks as the shell hits the steamer dead-on, snapping it in two. The smokestack releases one last tidy plume of white smoke, and within seconds, it is buried in the river, with the rest of the boat, gone.

Gritting his teeth, disbelieving and crying at his pitiful good fortune, he stares at the perturbed surface of the river. *You deserved it*, he whispers. *You bastards …*

* * *

... *You fucking nigger!* the madman shouts. Arms and legs like pistons, waving and flapping as he moves, he screams, *Fuck you, cunt! Get the fuck out of here!*

As the madman jostles past him, he wonders for an instant: *Is he talking to me?* But only an instant. He is neither black nor a woman, but he is sure he was the one being addressed, because people are cruel and stupid. And his breath catches, the padded shoulders of his jacket bunch. A year he has been here, and bitterness is all he knows, a literal taste in his mouth, like rusted steel. He is alienated by this Chinatown that resembles a brawling ghost, the store owners who throw down his change, the matronly waitresses who grumble obscenities when he asks for another pair of chopsticks. A few nights before at the Buddha Bar, as the local men puffed ferociously at cigarettes and unbuttoned their shirts down to mid-chest, a Chinese woman approached him: *I've gained so much weight since I came here. I'm fat because I'm lonely.* And she was right, she was plump and spent. Several times more she told him: *I'm lonely. I'm lonely.* He despised her hopelessness, so akin to his own, and when she made a last grab at his arm he ripped it away and walked out.

And now it seems he must share this futile city with the man who has just swore at him. His money pays for the man's drugs and alcohol, the man's insults. He can smell his piss in doorways, he is hounded by his stink. A full life is already behind him, and still every day he must work harder for less, and anything he does wrong will be taken down, used against him, worse than prison. At least in prison there is food, daily purpose, daily needs, a foreseeable goal: the day you are out. Millions starving in Asia, forced to sell children, use their children as beggars, prostrate on the street, their smudged little hands held out. But this madman who has done nothing with his life wanders free, swearing, spreading hate, along with the others who yell ugly, gurgling, dumb-stupid curses.

Another instant, a pause between maddened heartbeats, he thinks: *Crazy people say things they don't understand.* But the instant passes, and he is overwhelmed by the conviction that even a madman should know the difference between hate and not-hate. It should be hard-wired, coded just so, and he is sick of it not being so. So often.

He runs down the street after the madman, who continues shouting at the sidewalk: *FUCK you! FUCK you!* He catches up to him on a tree-lined avenue, and without warning, strikes him on the back of the head. The man goes down, his grotesque rags and filthy body much more presentable in the shade, and now deathly silent. Even this small victory is not enough. He begins kicking, everywhere, the neck, the back, the buttocks, the arms, legs, mottled in shade and sun. He kicks until his big toe is numb, and yet he continues, because he sees no blood, and the body on the ground seems as soft as a bundle of pillows ...

* * *

...The straight-A student rises from bed early each morning, not because it is required, but because he likes to do it, just as he likes studying, just as he likes it when his parents pat him on the head, or when they talk about a career in engineering, or perhaps medicine, or maybe even the law. He readily agrees with them when they tell him the girl is nice, but not necessarily ideal, since she is a musician and how much money can a musician possibly make?

Or when his friends invite him on a skiing trip, and his parents remind him that the SAT is next week—no further explanation needed, he is in his room, eyes bleary from computer screens and desk lamps. But he continues to rise at 7 a.m., catch the school bus on time, attend church on Sundays in a clean Oxford shirt and Doc Martens, watch movies with his parents, and contemplate a future wherein a nice Chinese American girl with willowy shampoo hair, a good complexion, someone who doesn't think Chinese men uncomfortably remind her of brothers and fathers, will marry him.

And then, the realization: he is too good. At everything. And with that a niggling little itch is inflamed to world-shaking proportions. There must be something more. And there is. Slicked-back hair and long baggy jeans. High-topped sneakers. Constant motion, mouth chewing gum, shoulders and hips swaying to imagined beats, fast cars that leave rubber tracks on the well-kept, glittering concrete. Fake IDs at bars, the invigorating muffled crunch as the baseball bat hits a warehouse window smothered in duct tape. CPUs sold on the local black market, in Hong Kong. Supply and demand, baby. And before long he owns turf. He notices the local girls in their short skirts and bronze legs. He is living the life, crossing the dividing lines between gangs, the Joe Boys and the Wah Ching, the karaoke bars submerged in cigarette smoke. Hair dyed to the tint of burnt siena. Flight bomber jacket, with all the right unit patches. Hookers with pussies so cavernous, so splendiferous, and he realizes that he studied all that SAT vocabulary and those great works of literature for a reason.

One night, his running mates toast him, somewhere between the twentieth and thirtieth toast of the evening, and he realizes he must now toast the boss. Again. The routine has grown monotonous; to toast and defer and sublimate and plain, fucking flat-out *genuflect*—and then he realizes. This is yet another stereotype. The simplification of another idea.

So he relinquishes it all, the hair gel and the car with the tinted windows and the leather jacket and chains and sunglasses. But his old home has been sold, his parents have moved away. Out of shame, no doubt. So he blows his last wad of cash on a motorcycle, a Harley Davidson, there is no substitute, and soon he is a speeding bulleting on Route 5, destination Los Angeles, Hollywood perhaps, or maybe even farther, down to Mexico, to further adventures, get your motor running, head out on the highway. He is dimly aware this is yet another cliché, but the sun shines, his hair fans with the wind like a lion's mane, and he chews on the dust between his teeth, quite content to ride on, move on, muddle on, until all the archetypes and paradigms flee …

* * *

…*May 5, 1949—Train to Fujian.* The date and event preserved on a scrap of paper, the day his family fled the Communists. His parents always said he was the stingiest in the family. His brothers and sisters, whether they knew it or not, believed in infinity: endless supplies of sesame candy would fortify them, another pair of shoes would magically appear when the old ones were shot through with holes, and the heavy soiled coins everyone carried in those days would be replaced with exact duplicates whenever necessary. But he would hoard everything he ever laid hands on, even scraps of notes, all of them covered with dates and particular objects gained, sold, traded, or lost. Some of the childish ledgers remain, and he can flip to a particular day, read a notation, and catapult himself to the past. day *May 5, 1949. The pork buns.* The long train ride, on a day hotter than any summer. He and his siblings left with nothing but rotting bananas to eat, and they were crying, tears and breath reeking of fruit. You had to be completely conscious of your belongings—one lurch of the car or the rude nudge of a fellow passenger could separate you, maybe for good. Sometimes the trains were so crowded that all precautions were for nothing. You had to trust in chance alone, that the person who wished to rob you was as immobile and paralyzed as you were. That day he was shoved face-to-face with a shrunken old man with only one eye, and for hours he was forced to stare at the empty socket, the joyless crushed depths there. Sitting near the man was presumably his family: a woman and two children, all of them small, round, and utterly exhausted. On the floor next to them was a basket of pork buns. It might as well have been gold. Deep in the night, as snores ricocheted around the compartment and people mumbled to themselves in sleep, he stole all the buns and gave them to his brothers and sisters. They ate in complete silence, eyes casting about for anyone who might catch them. No one did.

He knows he is growing old, because he finds himself thinking of these things for no reason late at night. He thinks of the one-eyed man, wonders if the man and his family survived, or if he stole their last bit of food, destroyed their last hopes. He wonders if the crime was worth it. Then he looks across the dinner table at his son, for whom anything past five minutes old must be discarded, the lockstep movements of his jaw as he devours his food. He sees the old man's face ...

* * *

... and he urges his horse deeper and deeper into the woods, over slippery outcroppings of rocks, through canopies of leaves that are as lush as waterfalls, beyond the reach of sunlight itself. Three days he and his horse have traveled, and his hands are red and raw against the leather reins, but still the horse bristles, panting, white spittle draining from its mouth, pushed to the verge of collapse, but seized with bloodlust, as the man is.

And sure enough, as the moon soars overhead and his horse huffs cold air in a powerful double spout, he sees the flash of silk, a ripple where there is no water. Within seconds, he is upon her. Mischievous as always, she lounges on a slab, tapping fingers to stomach in a playful rhythm: *Bum bum, bum bum bum.*

His horse whinnies, and she springs upright, flustered and modest, a perfumed sleeve held to her nose and mouth, her eyes still. She communicates without speaking.

Why did you come?

He will not allow her the comfort of an answer. With a practiced hand, the bow is now up, the string drawn to his ear. The feathered tip of the arrow pricks his fingers as he waits. Again, she speaks without a word.

I meant no harm.

They never mean harm. Princess Yang Kwei-fei never meant harm, but a kingdom perished because of her. To be a man is to be susceptible to a woman, and to be a woman is to ruin the dignity of man. Their crops withered, their community cursed, the villagers have slung dirt in his eyes. His pigs have been gathered and slaughtered on the spot so the spiritual contagion would not spread. Their corpses jam up his doorway, decaying, useless. Even the monks—

those damn righteous monks—have shook their heads *No*, pushed him away from their temple gates with surprisingly strong, muscular arms. Since then he has traveled far, days measured by the effort required to drag his horse across a river, the number of mountains crossed, the times clouds promised rain but withered into unrelenting blue sky.

And now she sings a wordless melody, and he recalls the salty taste of her skin, the way the sunrise caught her face just so, the song she hummed as she prepared his food, the same as the one she sings now, but he realizes that it is only wordless because he cannot remember the words. He taught her the song, and she has stolen it from him.

And then the lyrics enter his life again as she sings them:

> *We told each other secretly in the quiet midnight world*
> *That we wished to fly in heaven,*
> *two birds with the wings of one,*
> *And to grow together on the earth, two branches of one tree.*
> *... Earth endures, heaven endures; sometime both shall end,*
> *While this unending sorrow goes on and on forever.*

His arms are trembling. Sweat stings his eyes. A new bedevilment? But she has nothing to do with it, it is the old song that is defeating him. *Shut up!* he hisses.

You only do this because you are expected to. Because they fear.

All very well for her to say that. She has no obligations, she can go where she wants, be with whom she wants, century after century. She blew out the candles for him every night, and in the gesture was a secrecy borne from the need to protect, control, devour. She has no ancestors to answer to, no craven magistrates with whip-like mustaches to appease. *To protect us all, you must kill.* That was what the mousy man proclaimed, and the words had been painstakingly inscribed on golden parchment which deserved a finer commandment.

Please.

The arrow flees the bow, a poor shot that embeds itself in the rock she is sitting on. She flees, her low gown blowing behind her. He kicks at his horse, but it is too late—the wearied animal sinks to the ground, in sections. He tumbles off it and hurries after her. The forest hurtles at him. Branches scratch his face, wide unseen spaces swoosh by. It is as if he has crossed the edge of the world and fallen off it. Still his hand grips the bow tightly. He can see the darting shade ahead, bouncing from darkness to darkness. She knows these woods, she knows where each rock and jutting stump and hollowed-out grove is. He must not lose sight of her, or all is lost.

And then, luck, as her gown catches on a tree branch. He stretches a new arrow across his bow, she turns, and he sees her thin face with that tapered nose, those jade eyes, full-on. She communicates:

I am not special. Nothing is special to me except—

The arrow is precise this time. The shaft sprouts from her heart. Her mouth opens, and it as if the spirit within is being yanked away through there, escorted to the heavens. Then she sags to the ground, her gown disintegrating before his eyes, and all is dark. He falls to his knees, his bow slipping down among the deep tree roots, lost forever. He runs his fingers against the intelligent curve of her forehead, her snout still warm and moist, her luxuriant fur concluding in a tail that is bushy with fright, death. He gathers the dead fox into his arms and sits there, all sensation of place and time lost, and he tries to sing. Several times he attempts it, but not a sound, not a squeak can emerge. He pleads with the lifeless form to allow him to sing, and still he cannot remember the words. He will never remember. Despondent with grief he cannot accept, he sits in the coal-black forest, awaiting the sunrise, another dawn that can only herald death and forgetting.

* * *

A nature show is on the television. It is tragic that over forty Florida panthers have died in the last thirty years from collisions with cars. Actually, the more he considers the image, the more he is pleased with it: the handsome animal, the muscles in his haunches shifting between elegant tension and release as he charges the highway, straight towards fat, wide-eyed tourists in their sedans, knowing full well that he will die, that death is not all that important.

Somber, he thinks about what he has done (very little), what he can do (the same very little), what is no longer open to him (everything else). It would be nice to leave, to walk out the door of his apartment, to never return, to gain significance in absence. But he has responsibilities, co-workers, obligations. If he doesn't show up tomorrow, then this would happen, which would lead to that, and then this wouldn't work. Big mess all around. He must be reliable. Invisible yes, but indispensable, even if no one else notices or recognizes. One must be practical. One must accept boundaries. If everyone did what they wanted all the time, we would all be endangered animals.

Still, a trip would be nice. Florida or Hawaii. Pressed into a tiny jet seat with hundreds of others, coughing, recirculating stale air, unclassified bacteria. Removing sneakers and shoes for airport security. The faint distaste of bad foot odor. Forget it. He can do without that as well. The couch is much better. He dreamed something last night. What was it? He can only remember how he felt: potent, tragic, free. He chases after fragments of images, as awkward as one fumbling for shreds of paper carried by the wind. He does remember one thing. He is in the sky, not exactly flying—he knows flying means sex, or does it signify a raging ego, he forgets—more like floating. Borne into the night like a spirit, the mountains crimson and alien below him, and yet he was warm. He holds onto the feeling as long as he can, but the more he struggles to preserve it, the more it dissipates. Nothing is left now but the sour taste of his tongue between his teeth. He has decided. Changes will be made. Life will be transformed. Blood and guts required.

It has grown late. Amazing how one can lose desire, appetite, thought when the sun goes down. Tomorrow he must remember what he was thinking, the feeling that prompted those thoughts. Especially the feeling. But as he sinks into the comfortable folds of his couch, the only desire left is sleep. Perhaps there will be another dream, and it will be just as good as the one the previous night, or better yet, a little stronger, because that will encourage him all the more, and maybe provide the head start he needs. He must remember tomorrow, before dark. Lying in blackness, the television whispering to him, his eyes sagging shut, he hums something. He doesn't know where he learned it, but it comes out in a tumble, and the lyrics too, someone else's song.

Never was it thought I would return
So neighbors come over the garden wall

Every one sobbing out welcome
Then as darkness falls, by candle light
We stare into each other's faces
As if in a dream.

FLOATING WORLD
A Film Treatment

T*HIS IS NOT A TREATMENT IN THE STRICT, CUS-tomary sense. It is the sketchy outlines of a blueprint, the initial crunch of tires on asphalt as the car lurches forward with countless destinations in mind. With luck, this will someday be a film; with greater luck, it will become several films.*

Two locales: a city in the US, and a city somewhere else in the world. For now, say San Francisco and Hong Kong. Two cities mired in the present, nestled to ocean. Two cosmopolitan centers where appearance means much. Two insulated, insular entities that have not yet lost their power to attract and sway. Most of all, two places where every once in a while one can still find oneself on a hilltop, gazing through mist to watery lights below, irrevocably alone.

Five characters: Two men, three women. One man and one woman live in San Francisco, one man and one woman live in Hong Kong. The third woman is the thread that connects them all. Most crucially, the same actor and actress will play each pair. In other words:

1. *San Francisco man (For now, call him Paul) = Hong Kong man (call him Gun Duk) = same actor*
2. *San Francisco woman (Halley) = Hong Kong woman (Cheng) = same actress*
3. *The third woman (Miho) = present at both locations*

Why the duplication of actors? Across the world, parallel lives are lived. Many Pauls (or Gun Duks) may very well populate other cities in this world, or in other worlds. Similar in some aspects, different in others, and yet still reducible to a common core, even if the core is nothing more than a twitch, a prejudice, a longing.

Paul: Late twenties, disciplined yet noncommittal, genial but dispassionate. Daily life occupied with a task demanding punctuality, responsibility, professionalism. Managerial role perhaps, or therapist. A job, something to do well, nothing more. He is not one who secretly nurses a hidden talent—*No wallflower waiting to bloom here, thank you.* He is at peace with his lack of originality. Perhaps because of it, he is confident. Meeting women, making them feel at ease, sleeping with them, later disassociating himself from them as gently as one lays a sleepy child to rest at night. The elegant clink of the wine glass, to the closing of the bedroom door in the morning. Perhaps he plays a musical instrument, for his ears alone, even if female visitors demand a performance—*Sorry, forgot how to play long ago*—and later, in solitude, he finds happiness in his fingers roaming on the frets of his guitar, or tickling the keys of his saxophone.

Movement: The film's progress should bring transposition and juxtaposition. Hope gives way to resolution; complacency erodes to bewilderment. San Francisco is transformed from summer fog and bleached sunlight to winter's chill winds and rain that thuds on. Hong Kong struggles through the pregnant thunderclouds of August to arrive at the serene, spent skies of January. Beer coated with the neon of evening may dribble down Gun Duk's mouth as his friends chant away, daring him to finish the whole bottle; at the same instant, Paul vomits into the toilet bowl, seized with the morning hangover.

Gun Duk: Gambler to excess, his passion and crucible. Stocks, horse races at the Happy Valley track, even hobnobbing at the Jockey Club when opportunity allows. Besides that, he has no convictions, very happily so. Easy to say he never grew up, but there is more than that— he did grow up, and found it wanting. He cares about work inasmuch it allows him to play. His apartment was exact and new only five years ago, purchased before the economic crisis—now it is worth 60 percent less, and as if in response, the interior has grown dingy, damp, cluttered. His life here has been distilled to the nightly glow of his computer screen as he pores over share prices, and chats with his buddies and contacts on the phone, always looking for an in, an up, an out.

Cars: Bringers of changed fortunes and death. Perhaps Paul and Halley meet because she nearly runs him over one day (for she is an absent-minded driver). Cars are a sore point with Paul; they easily outrage his sense of fair play. Something as simple as attempting to find street parking, a police car skulking behind you, and the impatient cop, lacking anything better to do, snaps on his loudspeaker: *Move it!* Or when cars run red lights, a breath from mowing you down, so oblivious to your existence that your near-demise is known only to yourself, all this just so they can rush to stop at the red light at the next corner. Gun Duk will eventually lose his life to a light bus, one of those mini-vans that shimmy as they scream around the turns in downtown Wanchai. He will be fleeing his creditors, a tale of high interest and physical punishment, just a case of getting mixed up with the wrong boss. More specifically, the wrong boss's would-be girlfriend Miho. What emotions seize his face when he is caught in the glare of the onrushing headlights? Shock? Bemusement? Exhaustion? Maybe even acceptance?

Halley: Mid-twenties, relentless, boundless, and above all, honest. She has the drive to be a filmmaker, but no training or experience. Open-minded but inflexible, where Paul is close-minded but flexible. It has not been decided how they met—perhaps she nearly ran him over one day (for she is an absent-minded driver), and he was in an unnaturally forgiving mood. Or perhaps, seized with an idea for a film about psychotic therapists, she posed as a patient to pick his brain (*"It seems to me that you have, um, contradictory impulses..."*). No boyfriend, no time for them—they are too demanding, anyway. People talk about a woman's neediness and dependency, but it is always the man whining about the woman not being home on a Saturday evening. She simply cannot accommodate that sort of willy-nilly schedule; she may be struck with the desire to shoot the moon rising over Telegraph Hill, or spend the evening repainting her apartment for the third time this month. But at least with Paul, there are no expectations or obligations. She often calls him at three in the morning—yes, she has heard all the evidence that suggests that three o'clock is the soul's low ebb, but that is when she is calm enough to formulate questions. She only sleeps three hours a night anyway, like Thomas Edison, her hero. She calls Paul, he makes a show of grumbling, but he never hangs up. Mostly he just listens. A good listener is harder to find than good sex.

Further on cars: Paul has fantasies. A car will nearly run him down, the driver will drop his window for a crude remark in the midst of a one-handed cell-phone conversation, and he will reach out, grab the man by the lapels, and bodily haul him from the vehicle. The car will continue puttering down the street, rudderless, and finally come to a crunching stop against a wall, or a dumpster. In the meantime, he will have beaten the man's face to a satisfying pulp, after which he will find the car keys, drop them through the nearest sewer grating, and disappear like the breeze. All he wants is egalitarianism: *Everyone should be treated decently, all the time.* Or maybe he is simply an egalitarian snob: *You just want yourself to be treated well, is all.* Halley, too, is fascinated with the lawlessness of red-light running, and she spends her days filming such incidents. All makes, models, neighborhoods, social classes, ethnicities. Some run the lights with impunity, others get an aggrieved yell or the honk of an opposing horn. She has no idea what she will do with this footage, but she suspects it will have anthropological value someday. For now, she enjoys showing Paul these rough scenes and watching his face burn crimson.

Cheng: She heard all the stories about Hong Kong when she was a child growing up in China. She couldn't quite believe them until she was fresh off the train to Kowloon, riding a bus as it clung to the corners like a race car, sheer centrifugal force pinning her body and face to the window, the summer wind scalding her. She looked upon the dozens of faces in the street looking back at her incuriously, and she knew: *No place like this.* She had come to make a living, perhaps make it big, in what she had no idea, but in a place with millions of people, millions of ideas, surely there would be a few which she could synchronize with, like the hundred-strong crowds that march in lockstep across intersections. That was two years ago.

Habits: Gun Duk is addicted to Coca-Cola. Empty cans pile up in artless clumps in his apartment, even as Cheng constantly badgers him: *All that sugar and caffeine can't be good for you!* She is right, he knows it; he also knows that this is her function as his girlfriend, to point out these things. But Miho is different. She is old enough to know that vice is what it is, and should be accepted with a shrug. So Gun Duk and Miho spend a long evening sitting atop the railings overlooking Hong Kong Harbor, and the cans pile up at their feet, she in her short white dress and perfectly cut jacket, he in his crushed velvet shirt and Diesel jeans, the older woman and the younger man, neither of them demanding more than company.

Miho: Hard to believe that a girl from a modest snowbound village in Hokkaido could become a jetsetter. But here she is, an elegant woman who flits between Hong Kong and San Francisco: a new cosmetic line here, a fashion expo there. Flash bulbs pinpoint her in the crowd, young women take note of the purse she uses. She is in high demand: the middle-aged Hong Kong men with hair perfectly sprayed and parted on the side are always there. They are probably gangsters, with their mirrored sunglasses and their young cocky recruits bustling about to ensure convenience and comfort. And still, through it all, she remains unflappable, amused. Her politeness is a shield that even the hardest Big Boss is reluctant to test. But still, these Hong Kongers are so excitable, so lively. She is content to drift along with it, attracting all the free banquets and rumors.

The first meeting: To Halley, fashion means nothing more than throwing on a white button-down shirt when the occasion calls for it, but a friend of a friend is in need: can she help film a fashion show at the local gallery? So she drags out her pocket HD camera, not the high-quality 3-CCD model she owns, because to her this is merely a quick and compact formality. But maybe something subconscious is at work—her best-filmed moments occur on the pocket camera. And sure enough, as she glumly films the models, collagen pouts and Botox foreheads amid spotlights that dance like an epileptic attack, she sees Miho in the crowd. The older woman is completely still and attentive, the tip of a pen poised at her lips. She's one of the designers, she is told, and as if by magic, Miho turns to face her, from across the room, and nods a *hello*, as if they are old friends, or sharing an innocent secret. *Wow*, she thinks.

Halley: Lives in a studio apartment, but "shoebox" is more apt. She has not held down a job for years. She is not rebellious or political or incapable. Jobs just slip away from her, like soap through fingers. Her dresser is stuffed with speeding tickets, and unbeknownst to her, a warrant is out for her arrest (she has escaped through blind luck: typo in her official address, Emerald Cove Bay instead of Emerald

Lane). She is dimly aware that she has fines to pay, but they are mere cloudbursts, something to be momentarily frowned at and forgotten in the next moment's thrall. She is more worried about her significance, her duty to life and art. Is it possible she lives in a diminished age? She has heard older people speak of the good old days, the time of world wars, when life and people were meaningful. She despises even the suspicion that their talk is more than generational condescension.

The first meeting: The air at the Hong Kong Jockey Club is smeared with perfume and cigarettes. A favor has been called in with a racetrack connection, and Gun Duk is mixing at an evening banquet, all agog at the jewelry, the tuxedos, the blinding dinner plates. An older woman—Japanese, he suspects, by the way she seems to be perpetually bowing even when she is completely still—is fending off the advances of a local boss. Bullethead, the locals call him. Dum-dum bullet is more like it, he muses, with that ever-widening body. Now Bullethead has one hand on her shoulder, and his long rubbery lips are homing in on her face. She is playing the embarrassment card, turning her head away, straining to break contact, and yet Bullethead edges closer for the unwanted kiss. So with the ease that comes from navigating claustrophobic dance clubs every night, he slides between them. *How are you!* he beams at the older woman. *How long's it been?* And with that he sweeps her away, and is startled to find that she moves in perfect time with him, not even a missed step or gasp of surprise. *Do not worry,* he says in halting Japanese. *It's okay,* she answers, in creditable Cantonese: *Thank you.* They both laugh at the exchange, and then trade names. *Gun Duk. Miho.*

Gun Duk: Outside that miserable apartment, he is in love, with everything. The double-decker trams that drag him dinosaur-like through Causeway Bay to Wanchai, where he lives. The clubs where the English and Americans hang out to snort their cocaine (he has no interest in all that, but finds those *gueilo* fascinating nonetheless). The wispy arms and even wispier hair of the girls who populate the dance clubs. The smell of hot, greasy food at three in the morning as he and his buddies stumble home from another night of betting and carousing and singing.

Cheng: Perhaps she will be a writer. There is something writerly about this summer thunderstorm, and she wishes to capture it on paper: the fearsome beat of the raindrops against the windows, the uncollected laundry twisting in distress on the lines outside, the way the light seems to inhabit the tousled bedcovers. She and Gun Duk have been together for a year, and now he tsks-tsks at her: *Don't you clean your feet anymore? Look at this dead skin!* She is laid out on the tiled floor, the sweat on her exposed arms and legs slick as oil, and he rubs her feet, watching intently as the snowy specks of epidermis drift to the floor. To her, he seems both protective and distant. *What do you do when a man who cares for you, a man you love, is getting bored? First you must pinpoint what bores him, and how do you do that?* Much simpler if he could only say: *Sorry, I'm not interested anymore.* But no, he remains, even as she searches in vain for a job, and he patiently points out the best local noodle shops, or the latest in Hong Kong slang, or how to get from here to there. And he still buys her those perfect-fitting jeans (*such a compliment that he studies my body that carefully*), those zip-up leather boots. Maybe he is waiting for her to declare boredom first, like the opening gambit of a chess match. But, she sighs to herself, it seems so impossible, with such a cramped yet cozy ceiling above them while the rain runs riot outside.

Similarities: One can read Gun Duk as the path in life Paul never took, or vice-versa. Both needing to be awakened, both unsuspecting and walking towards crisis. Cheng and Halley, on the other hand, regard the world with clear-eyed curiosity. They are ready for adventure, and even to depart this world if necessary—or more accurately, to cross from one world to the next. Neither doppelganger will meet the other, but they will become dimly aware of the other's existence.

The moment: Halley has made herself up for this occasion, but plainly she is no expert—this Miho sees when they meet at the Italian café for dinner. With that overemphasized eye shadow and ruby lipstick, she might as well have been a circus clown. But Miho discreetly ushers her to the bathroom for a quick makeover. First Halley wipes off all the makeup as best she can, and now she looks like a doll left in the rain, but it doesn't matter because Miho is saying in that charming Japanese accent, *I saw your short film. I think ... very good.* Halley gasps: *Really? Yes,* Miho answers, ever precise as she applies some subtle mascara— the Japanese know how to hide their imperfections with the minimum amount of application, she had explained earlier. *You should come to Hong Kong,* she continues. *I know some people. You can make a film there.* Halley hems and haws and Miho mistakes it for reluctance: *Oh, I am sorry. Maybe you have boyfriend here?* No, no, of course not, Halley assures her, *No way, men are like kids.* Miho nods once, emphatically, like a schoolgirl satisfied with the adulation she is receiving.

Yes, I agree. No husband for me, too. No more needs to be said; they both know that they could recount the same stories, and arrive at the same conclusions. So instead they both laugh. And then Miho frames Halley's new face in both hands and presents it to the bathroom mirror. Halley holds back her astonishment—it is as if they are the same woman, only fifteen years apart. And a few minutes later the thought overtakes her, as the waiter refills her coffee and she drinks distractedly, scalding the roof of her mouth. *I must be in love.*

Paul: He believes there are two kinds of men—men that others talk about, and men who others talk to about other men. He claims residence in the latter camp, but unbeknownst to him he also qualifies for the former. His ignorance of that contributes to his charm. He is decent, helpful, but untested. An entire evening spent listening to horrendous stories about friends who have been unemployed for *years,* or lovers with leukemia, or relatives arrested for arson—this is as far as he goes. He refuses himself any deeper contact with misfortune, angst, trauma. Still, when Halley comes a-calling at three in the morning, something in the sound of her voice is balm. Usually she's too preoccupied to even bother asking how he's doing. No dissimulation here, she is who she is, and that is something to be admired. Then there was the time they were sitting in the park, for that is what city people do; they sit and drowse and let the sun hit them full in the face, like junkies just before the headaches begin. Halley was having a moment, about a woman named Miho, and no facts were divulged, yet the tremble at the corner of Halley's lip suggested that an outburst was seconds away. So Paul did the only thing he could think of: he offered his shoulder. This was not easy, for Paul had poor excuses for shoulders—or as an ex-girlfriend told him once, *You can't even put one stork on your shoulder*—but still, he offered, and Halley laid her cheek there, and soon she was laughing about how her face was going to slip down his arm. He was too rapt with the idea that he was making himself useful to reply.

Suspicion: As a child, Miho was sick once, for weeks. Drifting in and out of fever, she remained in bed, but her dreams were life-like. Cities with heaven-high skyscrapers and avenues that stretched for miles, seaside towns lit by tavern light at dark, farms in the country where she could hide herself in the growing wheat and whisper with the crickets all night. She could see herself in all these places, or at least versions of herself: maybe shorter hair and simpler clothes here, maybe braces on her teeth there, maybe even a scar or two from unremembered accidents. And then she finally became well, and these flashes of almost-memory subsided. But every so often, during a trip, or upon meeting a person, she thinks, *I know this from somewhere.* Or: *You remind me of someone.* One evening she and Gun Duk ride the ferry to Cheng Chau, all the better to avoid attention, and eat at a cheap restaurant by the harbor. As they eat, she notices a young woman standing in the distance, lone under the streetlamp, watching them. *Dammit,* Gun Duk hisses. *It's my girlfriend. Sorry, I'll be right back.* And so the lone figure under the streetlamp becomes two, and Miho presses her face to the restaurant window, straining to look. *Is that young girl ... no, it couldn't be, impossible.* Before she can even breathe *Halley,* Gun Duk pulls the woman aside, out of view, into darkness, not to return.

Gun Duk: His weakness is envy. He sees all that

others have, the slick designer suits and the latest BMWs (Mercedes are too staid for him). Just when all seems right, something better dodges within his eyesight, just out of reach. He treats lovers (lately, just one lover) with consideration, generosity, even tenderness, but he refuses to give away all of himself. If he should change his mind, he reasons, if he should find someone better, why add to the hurt of the breakup with memories of total commitment?

How does it all begin? We see doors swing open onto a field of glistening green, only to watch the ground torn to bits the next moment as the horses storm out at the opening bell, the latest race at the Happy Valley track. Tight close-up on Cheng and Gun Duk among the spectators. She looks at him intently, choosing words with care: *I've heard about a tortoise statue that defies gravity. Every year, it climbs a little higher on that hill in Shatin, a few centimeters at a time, and people say that when it reaches the top, the world will end.* She waits for an answer. His slender musician's fingers white about his betting slips, he yells *Yeah!* just before the horses thunder around the bend and drown him out, her out, everything else out.

Or: The plastic blind sticks as it is raised, then gives way with a harsh squeak. Through the jet window, a new dawn breaks over the clouds. The sun works its way very slowly across Miho's face. With the sleepy puzzlement of a newborn, she looks around her—yes, that's right, she is on a jet, she is somewhere between East and West. Must be morning—it has that aqua color to it. Funny how she always falls asleep at night, and awakens in the morning. It is almost as if she has exchanged one universe for another; a land of perpetual black for this thrilling new territory of daybreak. She holds her hand up to her face and sees the veins glow red in the morning light. What would happen if she stayed on this jet and it flew on forever, floating between one dimension and the next, life and existence unspooling in countless directions beneath her?

Or: We see a television monitor that engulfs the entire frame. It is completely black, but it gradually fades in on Halley (or is it Cheng?). She is gazing at the floor, in subservience one would say, or perhaps contemplation if one is optimistic. She raises her eyes to look at the camera, at us. Deep dark rings rim her eyes, and they are red from exhaustion, or crying, or epiphany. And then we see an upturn to the corners of her mouth, and the smile works her way up to her eyes, until they have premature crow's feet. It is a smile of resignation, and yet it seems to reassure us: *It'll be alright after all.* And then the camera turns away from the monitor to focus on the man for whom this video is intended, ghost light scattered on his face. He, too, is tired, and the stubble on his chin is as gray as an old man's in the unforgiving glow. But instead of a smile, we see the shine of tears in his eyes. It is only later that we realize that this is Paul, and he is watching Halley's goodbye, her testament.

The last of Halley: She wanders the streets of Hong Kong, alone, her hair tousled, her clothes slept in for days, a backpack sagging from one shoulder, her pocket camera from the other. If not for the camera, one could easily mistake her for a homeless person. She looks up, past the soaring spires of downtown Central, to the breaking of sun just over the manmade horizon. She has lost everything. She cannot go back to the States; she cannot find Miho. Freedom has brought nothingness. But she is here, she can feel her tired joints even as she stretches her arms and lets the light happen onto her face. There is another place to go, different people to meet. Or perhaps they are all the same, because she believes that in life, you meet the same people over and over—they may be more or less developed, but they are more or less similar. And in another place she will meet another Miho, and this Miho will say, *yes*. Staggered with the hope, she clutches the camera against her heart, her eyes squeezed shut with the intensity of the thought. And then she is gone.

In bed: Cheng and Gun Duk, both naked, face each other, but Gun Duk is asleep. She says his name, but he refuses to stir. She arranges his hair so that it falls in a boyish sweep over his eyebrow, and reflects on the shame of aging. Not for him, not ever, please. She whispers, asking him if there is someone else, knowing full well he cannot hear. He doesn't answer, but the breath of her words on his face awakens him. *What?* he mutters, but her lips are on his now, and she holds him tight, crushing him to her, wanting to shut off all response and dissent and failure, as he kisses the jut of her shoulder blades.

Cut to: The carnal screams of a woman, extreme close-up on her mouth as her voice echoes in the cavernous space, the video pixilated and all but unreadable. *Yes, that's it … deep, deep.* Moments later Halley is leading Paul out of the Market Street Theatre. He is zombielike, more than a bit embarrassed. She is thoughtful. *Do you really think it's possible to make that kind of sound?* she asks. *The* thwap, thwap, thwap? She pats herself all over, trying to reproduce it, but he silences her with a wince. And yet, he enjoys playing this role of squeamish skeptic. The fact is, yes, that sound is possible, and he's heard it many times, firsthand, but damned if she is going to squeeze that information out of him.

Cheng: Sometimes she wonders if she loves Gun Duk merely because he was the first man in this city to love her. No, he has a good heart, she still believes that. Even when he is annoyed by her, even when he comes home late at night rank with nicotine and beer, she never thinks he has cheated on her, not for an instant. When she is upset, when she has a rotten day working another temp job as a clerk or secretary, when she feels the skeptical eyes on her because she is just some clueless nitwit from the countryside, when the words *MAINLAND CHINESE* may as well be branded on her forehead, he can detect her mood without even a word on her part. And then his arm wraps around her waist and he holds her, both of them still and silent. Maybe it is her own fault that she is losing him, she thinks. What can she offer besides a good lay now and then, and endless trouble, the pressure of providing for two people? It would be easier if she was just someone else, someone who would remember everything that happened up to now, but gifted with different circumstances, different abilities, a myriad of ways to show appreciation.

Disappearances: Absence and presence are constantly at war. Miho is in San Francisco, and then in Hong Kong— wherever she is not, she is missed. Cheng awaits Gun Duk in that decrepit apartment, and finally, one night, she waits and he does not come. She walks the city, entertaining the faintest of hopes that she will see him. And then a miracle, for she does see him, sprinting down the street, as easy as a native in the jungle, people standing in for trees and bushes, Bullethead and his buddies in pursuit, brandishing meat cleavers like incompetents from a comedy movie. Then Gun Duk sees her, and cuts into the street in her direction. In the center of the road, another miracle: Gun Duk sees Cheng on one side of the street, and on the other, Halley. He freezes, for an instant, and the instant is shunted aside with the screech of tires. One moment he is there and in the next he has vacated the space where he was. Across the street, Halley, jet-lagged, aimless, sees the back of the minibus, hears the tires, and a moment later a young man spat out by the bus's passing. Instinctually, she jams her button down on her camera's candy-red RECORD button and films what is left of the young man on the road. Something about his face is familiar. Still, the sight is too horrible and her gaze floats up, to across the street, looking but not seeing, and then she sees. She is looking at herself—or rather, she is looking at someone who looks like her, except that the other woman has different hair and clothes. The other woman is staring down at the dead man who looks like Paul. The cold-blue light from a police car scores Halley's vision, and after she is done blinking, she looks across the street. The other woman is gone.

More disappearances: Likewise, one night at three o'clock, Paul does not receive a call from Halley. She has left the country. He traces her to Hong Kong, and it is discovered that she saw Miho there briefly. What transpired there, no one can say, at least not immediately, but shortly afterwards, she vanished completely. All that remains is a videotape. The central mystery of the film is now in play. Paul must go to Hong Kong, even if it means shirking responsibilities. He must know what happened. Cheng must know about Miho, even after Gun Duk's death. Will

the two of them meet through Miho? Will their mutual
search lead them to Hokkaido, to a snow-scoured street
in the pregnant silence of winter, to Miho's home, where
Miho has been incapacitated with another bout of fever?
What will Paul and Cheng say when they see the mirror
image of their missing loved ones in each other?

Miho: She finds San Francisco to be a fearsome place,
with all these smiling people, all their pretty talk, all the
adroit avoidance of commitment. Appointments are hinted
at, vague promises made, and nothing happens. As she
takes lengthy walks down the deserted avenues, it seems
to her that this place is the beginning of a city rather than
the real thing. Turn a corner, and the thriving traffic and
bodies, the lively rot and decay, are nowhere to be seen.
But Halley *is* the kind of city person she is accustomed to.
She is unadorned, honest. *I'll meet you at seven,* or *That's
a beautiful dress,* or *I promise I'll do it: I won't forget.* She
means all of it. How could such a woman live in this town?
Those who cannot commit always prey on those who can.
Miho feels she has to protect this young woman, somehow
preserve that integrity. She thinks: *That poor Halley, maybe
she has a small crush on me. Gun Duk, too.* He is so wayward
and cocky and yet always ready for a drink, for conversation,
for friendship on demand. She wishes she could love them
in return, but love disappeared from her long ago. Maybe
it left with the sickness of her youth. Maybe that is it—she
recognizes in them her own childhood, when she, also, was
too decorous or romantic to make a full confession of love.

The dancer: She is a folk dancer who is also trained in
the modern idiom. In bare feet, but with the blossom-like
satin robes and braided hair of Chinese princesses past, she

twirls as the sound system throbs with a melody that could belong to either East or West. One can easily accept it as a Verdi opera, what with that lush symphonic arrangement, but it also has the plaintive austerity of an evening spent alone in a pagoda, on an autumn lake. Likewise, her downward look suggests repose, reticence, elegance, but then a sudden twist of the arms or a forthright step betray brash modern confidence. Paul watches her spin and soar across the mammoth museum auditorium, and wonders: *Have I seen her before? Maybe in a past life.* In Hong Kong, the same dancer performs the same routine in the Exhibition Centre, a spotlight staying on her with unerring precision. Cheng observes from a distance. She, too, has a premonition: *This dancer knows something I don't. Something vitally important.*

The karaoke house: It is late, and Halley is drunk. Miho has left the US once again, uncertain of a date of return. *I didn't even have a chance to hang with her*, she sighs. *Do you even know if she ...* begins Paul, but she refuses to let him finish the reasonable question. *My love is away, and I'm upset about it*, she slurs. *Now I will sing.* Paul winces, a genuine wince this time, because to him karaoke is a betrayal, a surrender to conformity. They are huddled together in a private booth, a disco ball faltering above them. As a postcard-plastic moon hangs on the television screen, she launches into an old Flamingos song: *The moon is bright ... and so am I ... many millions of people pass by ...* She is slumping against him now, fighting her drunkenness, entirely focused on finishing this tune as if something good will come out of it, and even as he crosses his arms and thinks, *I can't believe I'm here*, he watches her. She does have a good singing voice, even when drunk. In fact ... *But they all disappear from view* ... She pours out her soul, oblivious to the man she is leaning against, and as he stares at her, transfixed, breath trapped in his throat, mouth gaping, gripped with a newborn urge to put his arm around her shoulders as she sings of having eyes for someone else, he thinks to himself: *Oh shit. This is love.*

GHOST WIFE

IT STARTED WITH THE STRAY DOG AND THE woman with the missing scalp. This was over fifteen years ago, when he was fresh in Beijing, back when he was pretending to be a journalist but preferred to think of himself as a *wanderer*, writing for the first in a succession of expat newsweeklies, content with the change of pace and the cheap beer. His photographer buddy had gotten word of a woman who had been attacked by a dog: *Dude, her scalp was literally ripped off.* Perfect fodder for a piece he was writing about the wild dogs in the city, and the health-safety risks. A favor in return for a paid lunch later, he was in her room at Haidian Hospital, at the corner of Zhongguancun Street. This was long before the Olympics, and Zhongguancun was still a pretty two-lane road with a line of trees down the middle.

He was prepared for gruesome: missing eyebrows, a cocoon of bandages, maybe. Instead he saw square little glasses perched under intact eyebrows, a full head of hair—originally dyed red, now going rusty from hospital life. Her English name was Mercedes (like the car, she explained with great seriousness), and she first mistook him for a Korean (a common reaction) but when he told her his family was originally from Sichuan, she was happy to talk. Yes, a stray dog had attacked, bitten her scalp clean off. She had to chase it for two blocks to get it back. After that she'd walked into the hospital, scalp in hand, calm as anything, and asked if someone could sew it back on. One of the nurses, probably thinking she was a ghost, had fainted dead on sight. It was unnatural, how Mercedes was so blasé about it. Like this was how life was.

That would have been that, except she then asked him about post-1966 Beatles and Bob Dylan. Due to the Cultural Revolution, none of that stuff had made it out to China, so she'd completely missed out on Dylan going electric. Her question had to be a sign, because earlier that day he had been thinking of rewriting "Back in the USSR" for China: *That Mao-Mao-Mao-Mao-Mao is always on my m-m-m-mind…* He was only a dabbler when it came to music, and yet as he explained, *Blonde on Blonde, The White Album* and *Abbey Road*, something clicked in place inside him. That was the thing about living somewhere else—you get to be someone who isn't yourself, someone that maybe even someone else wants you to be, and like magic you become that someone.

Every time they met after that she would come up with an off-balance greeting. *I think I might become a mermaid today.* Or, *I'd like to move to the top of a mountain. Or live in a box on the street.* Like she reserved the right to be silly with him. She had the Buddhist thing where she was certain she was being punished for misdoings in a previous life. Father hit by an official's car when she was a kid, gave him a bad leg for life, and in the messed-up way these things sometimes go, the local court ordered him to pay the official a huge fine. Her mom? She went crazy a while back, but the local asylums weren't fit for a wild dog, so she was confined to her bedroom at home, screaming and stomping all the time. Living in a city where monitoring the smog was an international pastime, did she suffer from asthma? Of course. *A Mercedes with a bad engine*, she said. He told her he wasn't going to be scared off. He was happy to absorb some of her bad luck, and he told her so. Where did this sickly sweet gallantry come from? Damned if he knew.

She was a grad student, pinched and almost spindly, and she missed nothing. He learned to be comprehensively honest around her. This was new. He had become accustomed to a nudge or two towards hyperbole about himself, to glossing over a fault. But her calm, her bluntness, seemed to inspire the same from him. Whenever he had an ugly American outburst—like when they went to the pizza place, the pizza was shitty and the cashier refused to accept his credit card, and he yelled at them for a good five minutes—she wouldn't let him forget it, ever, yet she would always smirk when she brought these incidents up. In return he would tease her by suggesting she marry a pasty white guy for the green card. No, she was too principled for that. She would never get married anyway. She was reading de Beauvoir and wanted to be everything, man and woman, selfish and unselfish. How can wanting to be everything be unselfish? he would counter. And back and forth they went. Once she asked him point-blank: *If you hate this country, why do you stay here?* He was tempted to bring up the F. Scott Fitzgerald line about two opposing ideas and being able to function, but decided against it, because then he'd be treated to her rant about how much she hated Daisy Buchanan.

On a late October night, just after the summer heat broke, they raided a party in the courtyard of the Friendship Hotel. It was an anniversary celebration of some important something or other, but the true nexus of the event was the buffet table, resplendent with plates of roast chicken, baguettes and other Western bounties. He had two plastic bags with him, the filmy kind street vendors use to throw items into, and when people were occupied with a dignitary's speech they both stuffed them with as much food as they could carry. Too much: within seconds her bag burst, and bits of jelly and baguette and chicken spilled. Laughing, they ran, morsels on the ground marking their progress like Hansel and Gretel.

They stumbled through dim streets, over to a wooden shack just down the road from Beijing University. The Moon Café, they called it. Old newspapers were pasted all over the walls, a clear fire hazard with all the smoking going on, but for him they were a decent conversation starter because he could always find a recent article under his name. *There's my first piece—a language lesson. That advice column "Ask Ayi"? We took turns on that. I did the one about proper etiquette when it comes to fighting over the dinner bill.*

Tipsy and cozy on the bar's picnic bench, she said: *Do you know about ghost brides?* She went on to explain. In previous centuries, rich families with sons who died early would sometimes recruit young women to marry the son posthumously, so he wouldn't be alone in the afterlife. The woman would stay with the family the rest of her life, but would want for nothing. Nobody did that anymore—or almost no one, because a family had contacted her with a proposal.

You're joking, he said.

It's not a bad idea. Maybe I sacrifice, and it helps my karma.

That's ridiculous. Even if I believe you, which I don't.

She sighed. *You know China is so big that every story you*

hear must be true, somewhere?

Fine, it's true. Why do it? You have better options.

Maybe I don't. Maybe I'm not as smart or interesting as you think.

Then you're just a liar. A lying fox spirit.

Then why do you spend time with me?

He said, *Funny, I was going to ask you the same thing.*

She replied in Mandarin: *It's nice to spend time with someone who isn't tragic. This city is fucking tragic.* He didn't know where to take that so he just drank some more.

Three college students were squeezed in the corner table with guitars, noodling out Beatles songs. Pre-1966, of course. Too drunk to sit still, he approached them with three full beer bottles in hand: instant friendship. They were young all right, with a few stray hairs sprouting where beards should be. A rushed tutorial on the chords to "Come Together," and soon they were blues-ing it up, the bar patrons entranced by this burst of English song into their lives. He sang and hammed it, throwing screwy faces in her direction even though his vision had spaced out and he couldn't see her. It didn't matter, the intention was behind it. Intention was now behind everything he did.

Time compressed and eluded him after that. There was clapping, a lot of clanking beer bottles, and he and Mercedes were hailing a *miandi* mini-van taxi, even though they had no idea if it had a seat in back or not—some of them didn't. Luck of the draw, this one had a flat bench, and they had to hold onto each other as the van bounced and bounded. Her head was on his shoulder, then his was on hers, and then their heads would bonk and they would let out an exaggerated, laughing *Oh!* To her apartment first, except it was no longer her neighborhood, because the world around them was aglow with Soviet-era towers and sodium streetlamps. They were at a hotel; she was pulling him in. Fine, okay. He had to order a room. Show the U.S. passport. They wouldn't allow a Chinese citizen and a foreigner to share a room, so he rented two rooms. Both right next to each other. Somehow she piloted him in, and he was remarking very loudly that the place was quiet. CNN International on the TV, bed smelling of mothballs. Her hand was at his chest, steadying him. Actually her hand had somehow gotten under his shirt and she was massaging him and they were both lying on the bed next to each other, her red hair tickling his chin.

How are you feeling? she asked him.

He said, *I'm all right.*

Then you need more beer, she said.

Later, he asked her what she was reading these days. Bukowski. Not good. He didn't know a thing about Bukowski. And now she was reciting: *We're all going to die, all of us, what a circus! That alone should make us love each other but it doesn't.*

What about a trip to Beidaihe? he suggested. No one there this time of year, no Commie cadres on holiday to worry about—

That's not possible, she said.

Why? You gonna be busy marrying a ghost?

She stared at him. Then she said, slowly: *What would you say if I am a liar? Maybe the wild dog story is not true. Maybe I cut off my own scalp.*

I wouldn't believe you.

Some things are true, even if you don't want to believe.

Don't you know? You are what I say you are. You are what you think you are. That's how it works.

That's nice. But I can't believe that. Her hand was back under his shirt, fingers spread, moving up and down.

The next thing he knew it was morning, his head hollowed out. No sign of her. The bedsheets in the room next door had been ruffled, a bit. He had a fugitive notion that she had kissed him during the night, more than once. The TV had been on, because he was used to going to sleep with a TV on, and he remembered she was complaining about it because she needed complete dark and absence of noise to sleep. This was all he could recall.

She didn't have a phone at her family's apartment, and she never revealed her exact address (*I don't want you to visit, my parents would never stop asking questions if you did*), although he knew which building it was. For a few days after the Moon Café he toyed with the impulse to stand outside for a whole day, awaiting the moment he would see the flash of that red hair from behind the swinging front door. It would be something out of a Broadway musical. He wanted to compose a song about her, just for her amusement. He hadn't done that for someone since junior high, and even then he had merely stolen a Crowded House song and improvised some lyrics. A name like Mercedes though—that was just rife with possibilities.

A week later he heard about the fire. No consensus about how it started—a few people he interviewed later said a kitchen cooking accident had escalated. Others heard it had been started by a crazy old woman. Some believed it was a crazy young woman. Hard to remember correctly in all the confusion, and no one had witnessed the genesis of the fire first-hand. No physical evidence would settle the matter: by the time he arrived on the scene nothing was left save a few shriveled beams, a choking black cloud of smoke. The police weren't going to be helpful, especially to a foreign reporter. Crazy person might have started it? Impossible. Chinese people aren't crazy. He could have told them, *In China, every story, every possibility, is true. Don't you know that?*

Fifteen years later, the Moon Café still stands. The stereo plays Katy Perry now, but otherwise a lazy summer night is much the same as it was back then, with lopsided candles planted on every table, the time split between throwing darts and chewing on approximations of pizza. Expat newsweeklies have come and go, yet the old newspapers remain on the walls, and young journalists— make that *wanderers*—are more plentiful than ever, joined by local girlfriends and pals, spoken Mandarin and English all around and between, rat-tat-tat. In the corner, at his customary table, the grizzled veteran reporter sits, his hair wild and his goatee a bit too bushy. The young'uns look upon him with a mix of awe and suspicion. The things he must have seen! Back when Beijing had three ring roads instead of six! Even though the veteran is pleasant enough he is not one to initiate conversation, never brings company of his own. He prefers rum and Cokes over the watered-down local beers, and as he stares at his table, the same thought sometimes goes through all the young journalists' heads: *That's us if we stick around too long.* If they took the trouble to ask him what he was staring at, he could point out a fragment of an article preserved under the tabletop laminate housing a photo taken at random by a fellow journo some time after a friend had gone missing in a fire: a Chinese woman sitting on train tracks just outside town amid crumpled cans and bags, composed and looking skyward as if awaiting instructions, chestnut hair drifting in the breeze. He would tell you in all honesty that he is not sure if it is a woman or a spirit in the photo, awaiting a local train that will take her either to the afterlife or another story.

Litany, Eulogy

For Iris Chang

WE DID NOT WANT TO ATTRACT ATTENTION. America is a new place, my father told us, and it was best to merge, be no different from the others. Thus denim pants. Yellow plastic barrette in my hair. Braces to straighten my teeth. Once upon a time, our first home was an old brown building that reeked of janitor soap and gas. On a window sill broad enough for flower pots, my parents insisted on rosemary shrubs—good for cooking, good for keeping the insects away, good for shelter against everything except the people who lived above us. They blasted their music, *thump-ba-thump-ba-thump* rattling in my head, as if it was coming from inside me. They would toss their cigarettes out their windows and the butts would land in the rosemary, scorch holes in them, leave an after-scent that was like coal. My father collected a pail full of butts, that's how many they threw, and presented it to those upstairs people very politely, all Rodney King-like, can't we get along? They would slam the door on him, spit nonsensical Oriental-sounding words at him. And then I knew two things for the first time. First, this country is a battlefield. To win, you had to swell with aggression, and refuse to compromise. Second, my father was a coward. This conclusion didn't arrive all at once, but when he returned from upstairs in defeat, there was something in the way his mouth went slack that stayed with me, and later the image coalesced into a notion: *He is a coward.* Seven years old at the time, already burning passion, I yelled at those upstairs people to stop, chucked pebbles at their windows, but all that did was make them angry: *Shut up, ching-chong motherfucker!* I wanted to bust down their door, rip down wallpaper that I imagined was sun-bleached and sad, knock over furniture and belongings, tell them they were *assholes*, because I was a good girl, and I wasn't going to sink to their level and use the f-word. I recited this plan out loud, every detail, down to the *asshole*, and my mother heard. She slapped me in the head for bad language. Like the time I was trying to open a package of donuts, my hand slipped and I yelled *Shit!* She hit me then too, and for me the word *shit* means a bunch of powdered donuts scattering tragically to the floor. I fell flat to eat them anyway. You cannot waste anything, not a single speck of sugar. So I lapped it up, tongue to hardwood like a cat. And Mother, horrified, treated me just like a cat, thrusting her broom at me, and the straw poked me in the eyes, scratched my face. Yet later she was very reasonable, and said: *People who use bad language are out of ideas. You're smart enough to always have ideas. Always.*

The soldiers created a game out of it, I am told. A test to eradicate the coward inside you, vanquish every single fiber of being that does not allow you to attain your full potential. It was a diversion from the damn heat, the dust that stung their eyes, the sewers poisoned with dysentery and rotted limbs. If it had been winter, it would have been different. Snow to drink, water boiling all day and night. But in the summer, in the midst of drought, gas was rationed, hardly enough to even burn the prisoners' bodies. They tried, but the corpses could only burn halfway—the husks remained, blackened rusty gnarled trunks sprouting from the earth like contagion. Perhaps a tiny sliver of conscience remained in their souls, and the sight of the corpses was disturbing to them. So they created this game. Prisoners were lined up by the dozens, and the prisoners greatly outnumbered the soldiers, and yet the prisoners' eyes held only pleading, fear, supplication, which infuriated the soldiers all the more. *What an utter lack of pride and will and resistance— not even the desire to survive. Worse than animals.* The game would begin with the commander instructing the newly arrived conscripts: *It must be one swift, sure stroke. Observe!* And with that his blade swooped, a prisoner's head severed cleanly. Soon all of them were taking their turns, racing to see who would accumulate the most heads, the most accurate blows. The inexperienced troops couldn't get it right at first—heads would dangle from bodies, connected by flaps of skin, bobbling in place, and more blows were required to fully sever them. Through it all the prisoners never moved. They only trembled, cried out, muttered words to their gods in their own guttural language. *Shut up!* the soldiers would shriek, and they doubled their pace, just to quiet them all. Soon, inevitably, blood would run down the soldiers' faces and clothes, and it was strangely refreshing, even as the ground turned to mud with the blood and sank under their feet.

Tonight there is much ceremony and rejoicing, and thank you all for coming, I want to dedicate this on behalf of, without whom, thank you again. The waiters in their cute little half-tuxedos smile at me, and I want to ask,

How do you feel? Really? Business cards are passed to me: people's entire lives and reason for being condensed into razor-thin slices of 80-pound paper stock, a multitude of them in my hands. *Let's talk sometime.* I really cannot handle this responsibility. But nonetheless, I exhort my colleagues, give private little pep talks, *You should take on that job... I've heard about that diet and I think you should try it... Grab these opportunities, recognize how lucky you are.* I have written a single book, a straightforward chronicle of war crimes, and now I seemingly know everything. I leave rows of smiles in my wake, like tiny explosions. Pats on the shoulder, proper and friendly kisses on each cheek. Why am I here? Restatement: I know why I am here, but not the true *why*, because nothing has been done, nothing prevented. Events have been documented. That is all I have accomplished. In American society, there is no honor in merely observing. I am an instrument. Something blows a wind through me, my mouth moves, my fingers jump up and down like keys. I finish my fourth glass of wine, head throbbing, skin filled to bursting. Someone says, *What's your next masterpiece?* General laughter, as far away as the wind whipping through the exhibition hall's statue-gray courtyard. Above all, only one thought, stark as the flashbulbs that drone on ceaselessly, directed at myself: *You are nothing.* How dare I think that way, how self-absorbed, but this is not about me, this is about the thought, this is outside my purview, and I hold one hand to my head, the other to my mouth, not sure which one will erupt first, and all the while, *You are nothing you are nothing you are nothing you are nothing you are nothing you are nothing you are nothing.*

I catalog because this is meaning. What can be seen,

counted, pointed to—these are the things that matter. Three hundred thousand died, but then some claim two hundred thousand, and some even say barely anyone at all. Why not be inclusive and say *Far too many died.* Quantity shouldn't matter, but it does, because everything is not the same, we cannot tolerate *same,* there is no point to *same.* My set of tragic deaths is more important than your set of tragic deaths. A number becomes a story, statistical significance becomes tangible priority. What about the Yangtze flood of 1975? Over two hundred thousand people wiped off the map, and history was unaware for twenty years. But there must be a number. With a number comes responsibility, demands. *You must apologize for this, you must acknowledge this, it is criminal not to be cognizant of it.* With the crumpling and burning of a piece of paper containing research, a miniature bonfire, I could make it all disappear. The solar system explodes in eight hundred million years, and none of this will be of consequence to anyone.

Kill them all. That was the directive. The invading commander was disbelieving at first. Then it was all solid, a part of his life, like the ground under his feet. The order from Imperial Command was incontrovertible, with no hint of ambiguity. Still, he would have to communicate this properly to the soldiers. For them, the words would have no taste. But say the word *food*, in either the locals' tongue or the soldiers' mother language, and civilian and soldier alike would cradle their stomachs, look to the cloudless sky, mouths gaping, ready to accept anything. Then a short blessed rain, the grass going green for a triumphant week, and they all scrambled to collect it and eat it, some chewing on the spot, sprawled out like crippled snakes. Perched atop the city wall, underneath the shade of his immaculate umbrella, the invading commander witnessed all this, and with the trembling fingers of an artist, raked a cloth across his brow. He had come to realize how he would have to communicate to his men. And so a week later, the grass gone, the soldiers gathered in a restaurant bombed to a ruin, candlelight spastic on the walls. They fondled chopsticks and porcelain spoons, reduced to imagining, some of them clasping chafed hands over the flames, as if the fire itself was a great delicacy just out of reach. The commander said, *Food*, and the soldiers convulsed in reflexive response. *There is not enough of it*, the commander continued. *Too many people. There is only one way to remedy the situation*. This the soldiers could understand, and in the dim light their eyes danced, while in the distance the midnight watch sounded the bell.

The noise in my ear simply will not go away. It began a few weeks before, as I was handing in the proofs of the new book. I was thinking, *And soon this will be sent to Publisher's Weekly, The New York Review of Books, and it will be up to them*, and bang, there it was. Both ears, it would have been fine, but the sound limits itself to my left ear. It is as if someone is very delicately buzzing his lips right next to me. I slap at imagined insects, but nothing is there. I scratch at my face, not even near the offending ear—I simply itch all over. My skin is pockmarked with eczema. Perhaps it is the ear that is blessed, and the rest of my body cursed. This is an evolutionary trick. My left ear has acquired dog hearing, and the rest of me must catch up. I cannot sleep. I paint to pass the time: the daffodils outside the kitchen window, half-remembered horses from old oil paintings. Were the original paintings of memory genuine, or were they knock-offs from Chinatown? My friends say Chinatown food is terrible, because it is not authentic, but I say, *As long as it's good, who cares?* My five-year old son looks at some of my paintings. *What do you think?* I ask him. He grabs hold of my bony arm—I have lost much weight due to lack of sleep—and he says with great seriousness, *Are you okay, Mommy?* He looks so like my mother at that point, sharing her worry over me. And with that I realize that he hates the paintings. He thinks I have no talent, that my attempt at artistry is an affront, because otherwise he would say something, and instead he is making a vague comment about my health to hide this calamity.

The villagers had no time, I was told. The enemy was like a great wave, very natural, flooding down the hills in clumps, nothing symmetric about them. Fighting had gone on for some time, with many lost on all sides. At this point some only had knives, hatchets, torches. Others lacking even those had resorted to club-like substitute weapons. And now the enemy was approaching, and the villagers were informed: *You have one hour to leave.* That was all, no conditionals, no *or else.* Those who could gather food and clothes did—the rest only stared helplessly at their thatched roofs, their floors of dust and burned bits of twig. And on the hour, the enemy set fire to everything, many of the villagers giving up right at that point, sitting and watching the flames creep toward them, even gazing incuriously as their limbs ignited, and then they were screaming, but this was not their pain, not even their voices, this was just the act of a spirit escaping, or at least that is what the survivors would tell their children. Some ran out of their huts only to be immediately bludgeoned or shot. Others simply threw would-be escapees down the well, then tossed grenades in after them. Some of the villagers fled into the mountains, where the roving packs of wolves awaited. The razing of the town took place on a full moon, so for the first week afterwards, you could see the wolves from a distance, their eyes glowing like fire as they flowed between the trees, and when they set upon you, there was warmth and comfort in their hard breaths. You could appreciate their bright teeth, brighter than any human teeth you saw in your life, just as they sank into your neck.

I do not remember specific activity from childhood, only observations. Stabbing the tip of my finger with the record player needle so as to draw out a perfect bubble of blood—something as exact as that. The first moment I realized my father's breath was bad, or an awkward moment catching my mother in a state of undress, her breasts small and already drooping. There was so much sun, too much of it, and in those roads as wide as rivers, it shone down on you. In daytime my sister and I played hide and seek from it, and from each other. My sister with the bouncy head, and the arm I slammed in a car door once, because I was lazy enough to do it. Her face went all red as a result, and she never seemed more alive. An accident, I told Mother, and looked straight at her, blameless. *It all comes back*, she said. *Everything you do returns.* But no, the toad I accidentally flattened underfoot is not returning. My sister, even after lying flat on the bed, even after many trips to the doctor, does not return to me. She just moves on. Letters from school, letters from out of school, oh yes, she has left, something wrong with her, and it is not even her arm, it is with her head, all scrambled inside, like a dented pillow, even though it is by all credible appearances normal. I think that I should have slammed her head in the door; maybe that would have prevented this. Once, like a fool, I propped my feet on the handlebars of my bicycle, hands behind my head, and cruised. Then the school bus came at me, my feet dropped to the ground, and in the moment poised between standing and falling, I looked down at my left foot. The bus's tire shaved the edge of my shoe, an inch from crushing the toes. Then it barreled on, I was on my back, looking up at sky and brick buildings, and it was plain to see—I had used up my life. Everything from here on in was merely a favor.

My friends have commented on the state of my office, and usually their observation ends with similar sentiments: *This is intense. You should rearrange things. This can't be good for you.* Not a square inch of wall is bare—everywhere there are photos, laudatory notices, angry letters. I sit for hours as they gang up on me, and every so often a particular item sends me scrambling into myself. A book review written by a Chinese professor who never writes book reviews, but he cannot refrain from revealing how I have used doctored photos, how my facts cannot be correct, because if three hundred thousand people died, how did the population of this city increase by fifty thousand during this time period, and what about that map that was seemingly copied whole cloth from another source, a disreputable source? He is right. That is to say, I cannot focus on these particulars. The ache in my ear pounds like a drum every time I open my mouth to speak or desperately yawn. It's all I can think about now, but I have every right to be ashamed, because I have failed. They are all interested in statistics, credit, blame. No one asks about the *what*, the *why*, the *how*. They must focus on that miserable little author, which was not the intent. This chess game demanded more rigor, and through momentary weaknesses I have been undone. But I take solace in the photo of my father as a middle school student, so solemn and gawky, that is pinned in the corner of the bulletin board. He was a very quiet man, and yet what I remember the most about him is that very infrequent horse-like laugh he had. When my sister or I pulled an antic so outrageous, so distant from common sense, he would unleash that laugh. It was like history had erased itself and he was a child again, our equal. He must have been like that once, back in the homeland, before the war.

They killed you, but first they forced you to tear down your own house. Emplacements were needed, additional open space for traps and mines. Or perhaps the commander simply found aesthetic pleasure in empty ground. Any member of your family who could stand was expected to participate. To the children, this was a game, as every tragedy becomes a game; for them this was a tremendous lark, because they didn't have to go to school, because there was no more school, and this was just another event in a continuing deluge of good luck. They would pull nails, point them at each other like weapons, line them up in the corner in efficient little rows of five or ten. And you could only lean against the tattered walls and stare at them, and wish that everyone could free themselves from the need to grow, or understand responsibility. You wept into your smudged shirtsleeves at that thought, but still you were under orders to destroy, even as your arms hung tired and useless at your sides, and the soldiers beat your back with canes, but you did not feel a thing, for your body was one big callus. It was in your best interests to proceed slowly—the longer it took, the longer your own death was postponed. And yet progress was unstoppable, and you watched as shards of home drifted down the river, mixed with neighbors' detritus. Once the roof was down, the soldiers would spread lime everywhere, and at first dull outrage washed over you—*What was foul and polluted about my home?*— but this gave way to incomprehension. Why not assign this task to you? Was this some sort of unsaid apology? The soldiers grunted, muttered to themselves in their own language, and yet they were very thorough, even womanly, in their attentions. The powder would pile up, crystalline like snow, and the children would play in it, flinging it at each other, and now they were crying, for the lime was hitting their eyes, and all you could think is, *That's all right*, because the less they can see when the end comes, the easier it will be for them.

Some of the letters to me are more positive: *You should be proud for having brought this to light,* or *I saw you on that news program with my son—we were both too disturbed to watch it, but we respect you for your courage.* No, that is even worse, to know something but not to face it. Isn't it just another form of *not* knowing? Another failure. I have shoved a thing in front of a person, and commanded them: *Witness! Acknowledge!* I stare at a grainy photo, a woman in the midst of torture, a machete sickly sweet with death as it slices through her left ear. Two other men pin her down, and a strand from her braided hair falls across her wide-open face in a manner that might have inspired poets in another age. A soldier, perhaps the group's senior, stands apart from the tableau and stares straight at the camera, with neither joy nor horror on his face—only the placidity that comes from determination. This photo has traveled thousands of miles, been passed from one rebel's hand to another, eluded officials and censors, acquired the importance of a holy grail, because here was evidence, here was remembering. I saw it for the first time in a Chengdu tea garden, held in

the hands of an eighty year-old man with a beard that ran
down his chest and ended in a point just above his belt-line.
As he smoked and the birds rattled around in their cages,
he told me stories. About the great crossings of rivers, those
beautiful tremulous mountains he and his family discovered
even as they fled the invading armies, the cousin who was
kidnapped in those mountains by bandits, only to be set
free twenty years later and reunited with what was left of
his family. He offered me this photo of the soldiers and the
woman, and then he showed photos he had taken of every
visitor to that garden, locals and foreigners, everyone he
had had the privilege of meeting, volumes and volumes of
them, compulsion made history. He took a fresh photo of
the both of us, the camera stuttering out its timed click,
and gave me a thumbs-up as goodbye. Such an incongruous
gesture, but now it drives me to tears. Memories like these
and more crowd the office, and when I do fall asleep at my
desk, the nightmares come. My heart heaves in my body, I
believe this must be a coronary attack, and all the while it
is a mere rattle of fear because events are taking place out
of sequence, or reassembling into some opera, and it all
becomes clear, even in the sunny light of day when I wake,
face pressed to papers and decorated with ink: *I should have
lived then, I should have died then.*

The word *slave* wasn't used. Women who wanted to
stay alive accepted; those who refused were punished.
Not killed, although that did happen, more out of sheer
exhaustion than anything else, for the soldiers were still
hungry, still wretched in their clothes and skin, rubbing
dirty bare arms against dirty mouths, maddened by the
heat, and with all this, worrying about a woman was just
too much to bear. Often it was a matter of procedure:

if a woman wanted to walk down the street, she was allowed to, but not until after she had satisfied the soldiers standing sentry. Any movement, any glance that could be interpreted as reluctance or rebellion, was enough to drive them to action. And even as the women protested in their native tongue—*I did not say anything, I did not mean*—the soldiers grabbed their mouths, those spotless pale lips. How did they keep them so clean in this Hell? They pried those lips open, seized their tongues, and with the tips of their machetes, hacked them off, but the machete was not meant for such subtle work, and as a consequence, the downward stroke would slice open cheeks, necks, breasts. In every alley women lay, slumped and sitting on the ground in shock, staring at the items of their bodies left in the oven-like sun. Their eyes never blinked. They only looked down on their tongues, their breasts, their ears, as if they were secrets waiting to be unlocked.

How do you apologize? Start with one thing, then another, and finally you apologize for everything. That ends it for everyone else. Not very fair. In fact, selfishly unfair. As if you can take responsibility for something. And so the foreign minister blusters on TV, claiming to be responsible for my hearing problem and the knife cuts that I have inflicted on my own arm so as to calm myself. What a martyr you are Minister, it suits you, just as it suited me when I was nearly run over by the truck, just like my father when he slinked away from any conflict. But without apologies there is no point, is there not? So apologize; I insist. We cannot move forward in history without an apology. Everything else is insubstantial air. Better to deny, plausibly. Then we have reasons for doing something. He is not apologizing, so we must make him apologize. That is the mission. He knows this, and draws the game out for as long as he can muster. Then weakness or boredom sets in. We both forget, accuser and apologist, and then suddenly on a rainy day we see you on television, and you say *I regret, I am sorry, it is unfortunate.* And suddenly the game is over, and rain crashes down on the windows even harder.

When my mother died it was all very sad, I was told. A sudden illness. I did not have the chance to see her—I was participating in yet another conference, a chance to expound on the dangers of forgetfulness and neglect, *We must confront our collective pasts or we are doomed,* etcetera, and looking at these bright young faces, these assorted nods and clenched fists, I had to wonder, am I their Santa Claus? They gathered around me, offered chewed-up pens for signatures, and I signed, every last one, because I have no scruples about being a celebrity. Someone must set a good example:; it must be proven that to be famous is to be the same as everything else, just something to get through. *What you are doing cannot be measured.* Or, *The stories you are recovering will become part of our cultural narrative.* I can only mumble thanks, and suggest that the book will be around long after we are all gone. They can all get behind that. And then my sister calls: Mother has died. Strangely, I think Mother would approve of the fact that I was not present during her passing. Go forward, was her thing. The past is just an anchor. She never told us about her background. She was from a different country, so she didn't endure what my father did. She was in a rich family growing up, and somehow she was banished from her family, for reasons she never explained. She never talked about it, and neither did my father. They just moved on. The bliss of erased memory. Now I am executor of Mother's estate.

What are you going to do about the money? my sister asks. When Mother was alive, she sent my sister a stipend every month, and every month the same response: *How can I live on this?* And my mother would snap, *You don't have a job! You just sit at home, buy expensive clothes!* Which was true, although it wasn't my sister's fault, we were told, it was this thing inside her head, this thing that did not allow her to hold a job, that advised her to leave in the middle of a shift, or scream at people about cold coffee, but to my mother this was all just words, because my sister looked fine, and what was this thing inside her they kept talking about? If she really had something that dangerous, wouldn't she be dead by now? So my mother yelled, *Stop making excuses,* and my sister would counter with something about lack of parental affection when she was younger. And on and on, and now it was my turn to be Mother. Growing older does not mean more friends and wisdom—it means you must go to greater lengths to avoid people you no longer want to see. So I said to my sister, *I can't talk about this now,* and that was a big mistake. Neglect is fatal, and inattention leads to things like my sister stealing all the old family jewelry from my mother's cramped apartment, and the hatchback to boot, selling them for quick cash. Which is what she did. She didn't even use the profits for something daring like drugs. Instead, she bought strapless dresses that would be out of style six months later, or every variety of cigarette in the Western hemisphere, or a trip to Hawaii, even though she has been there fifteen times before with one of those ex-boyfriends who is married but can't seem to leave the picture, but it is the only place where she can "relax," and if I only gave her enough to settle down on Kona, and take that wellness class spiced with a little yoga, she would be perfectly happy, which is utter bull. *No snap judgments,* I say to myself to calm down, *you are no better.* But I am better, I have the earache to prove it, I am dripping with sympathy and compassion and respect for people who have long since died, and Mother has joined that pantheon. I sit awake at night under my fluorescent lamp, staring at the light until it dances violet in my eyes, regarding the numerous autographed copies of the book on my shelves, and I think that if I could burn these books one at a time, these shelves would eventually be bare, which is something to be looked forward to, but it also means the end.

You are a prisoner of war, and you are given a choice: You must bury the person next to you. Bury him alive, in the sand, up to his neck, and leave him for the winged predators and insects and high tides. Do it, or it will be done to you. What if the person is your next-door neighbor, the one you could never tolerate, the one who would spit on the ground when he walked, not caring about the barefoot children playing nearby? Kill him, and you are safe. No one would notice. His family is probably already dead. When this is all over, everyone who knows him would likely be dead. It would be a secret, between you and your captors. And you have been bestowed with good fortune, to receive this order. You could have been the victim instead of the perpetrator. Mathematically speaking, it could just as easily have been the reverse. So it really means only what you want it to mean, and the soldier in his burnished mustache is staring at you, eyes bulging like egg whites, ready to bark at you to *do it now.* You take the shovel and begin digging. That next-door neighbor is blubbering, driving you mad with his inchoate shouts and begging, and the soldiers beat him down with the butts of their rifles, and that only makes you dig harder, sand blistering your feet, slivers from the shovel handle jammed in your palms, sweat scalding your eyes, and you must dig deeper and deeper. All that is left is pure action, and maybe if you continue to dig, the order will be forgotten, or there will be a reprieve, or you will sink lower and lower into the pit you are building until you come out the other side, and all will be forgotten, like when you awakened after your very first night in this life. You will sleep and all of a sudden it will be thirty years later, and you will have a wife, and a daughter who writes books, and the daughter will ask you about the massacre, and you will tell her about burying your fellow villager, and now she knows as well, and must know more. You have passed down your affliction.

It was a blizzard, with youthful mispronunciation I called them *nor'eaters*, the snowflakes fat and lazy and beautiful, and my mother was yelling at me about something—no memory, only observation: her face spread out and giant, accusing me about a lost food item, one of many lost items. I never stole anything. I would appropriate, replace or hide or reformat, but never *steal*. She didn't believe, she never did. So she left to buy fresh groceries in her wisp of a hatchback, and on the icy road, just down the street from our building, a truck skidded into her. The entire passenger side of her car was crushed, she was pinned under the steering wheel, but all in all, she suffered only a busted kneecap. As the driver side window was bashed open to pull her out, bits of glass scored her face. The next-door neighbors carried her up all ten flights of stairs, gaining onlookers and followers as they went, footsteps and voices and shouts mounting those steps, *Take her to the hospital. No, we're taking her home first, she needs help, no she's fine we just need to get her medical card …* With that mass of noise and motion, it was a veritable social movement. My sister was off somewhere, trying to touch her nose with her bottom lip, and my father was at work. But my mother didn't utter a word. She wasn't directing anyone, no growls or complaints. She was being good for *me*. When the neighbors set her down on the couch, she just looked at me. The droplets of blood on her cheeks looked like cunningly placed makeup. She wanted me to fawn, to feel shock and relief and tears, to wipe that blood from her face, overcome with concern and love. I looked away from her, ran to my room. I was ashamed of her injury, her weakness, how this woman who yelled and screamed and prodded had been reduced to plain want. The neighbors stayed over, my father came home and spent the entire night at the couch, padding her fevered head with a cloth, and I watched it all from a sliver between opened door and frame. If I could, I would have stayed in that room for the rest of my life, because now I was regretting what I did, but it couldn't be undone, and my mother would always remember, every time I wouldn't look at her.

All I have left of my father is an interview about the massacre, preserved on VHS-C tape with lousy tracking. I set him up on the reading chair in the study, with a very distinguished set of books behind him on the shelves, in alphabetical order of course, Ronald Takaki to Walt Whitman. I didn't account for the shifting afternoon sun, so by the end of the session his face was scored with dapples of light through the window, reduced to white noise.

At first the soldiers wanted my mother, he says. His voice is flat, no emotion. He could be reciting vocabulary words at school. Maybe this is the only way he can tell the story, something as dry and factual as a history book. *But mother was pregnant, so the soldiers didn't want anything to do with her. Instead they dragged my aunt upstairs. My aunt decided she would rather die, so she fought back. They stabbed her, six times, once in the thigh, mostly in the chest, and they left her there on the floor. As soon as the soldiers were out the door, I ran upstairs to her...*

[Pause as my father shakes his head violently. In a voice that is vehement, blunt, completely unlike the impersonal tone of moments before, he addresses me, just the left of the camera: *Do we really have to do this? I don't want to do this.* I respond in a very whiny voice (but then I always think my voice sounds whiny): *Please Dad, this is important.* His stare clings to me for a good ten seconds. What is he holding onto? Fear? Guilt? Anger?]

I ran upstairs to my aunt, he continues, *and she said to me,* My heart hurts. Please get me some water. *I ran downstairs to find water, and by the time I got back upstairs she was dead. I was still a young kid and didn't have the strength to carry her out of the house to bury her, and my mom was in no condition to help. My aunt's body lay in that room for four days, and the flies were everywhere after the first day. My mother would sit over her around the clock, and shoo the flies away. Finally another enemy soldier came. He was an officer with glasses, and I remember that I could see the scratches on his glasses. He had heard about what had happened. He didn't apologize for his men, but he made a few motions with his hands, and I understood he wanted to help carry my aunt out to the yard. So we finally did. The officer left before I could ask him to help me bury her—it wouldn't have mattered, because I discovered that the ground was too hard to dig up. So we left the body out in the yard, and even more flies came. I can't remember what happened to the body after that, because other things started happening. But at the time I thought I was somehow responsible for her death, that she died because I was late bringing her the glass of water.*

[My father stops again and looks at the floor. *I never wanted to remember that*, he says. *Why did you force me? Why?*]

I have never seen his face like this before, and never will again. There is more to the tape, other stories, but all that remains with me now is his agony. The seed has been planted, in both of us—even though we never talked about the massacre again, all our future interactions were blighted by the weight of it. For the rest of his life, every time I addressed him he would shrink a bit, as if he expected me to say in my next breath: *Can you tell me more about the massacre?* Like I was a child who required unspeakable horror as my bedtime story.

I gave up on swearing when I was a child, but that was all right, for my boyfriend did all the swearing for me. He was not an editor or writer, but he was relentless. He would get up all close, his breath like rotten bananas, and yet this scent was comforting, as he would puff himself up with intensity, like birds taking flight: *Fuck it, you can do better than this. This part doesn't sing. Why do something when you don't try to be the best?* And then he would launch into the story of how he competed against this woman for his residency, and the woman looked and smiled like a cheerleader, a straight A student, except for that one time she got a B-plus, but that was because she was saving the life of a boy who got hit by a car the night before her final exam. How do you compete with that? But he did, and he won, by sheer exhausting persistence. In everything he did: Playing racquetball, grunting and throwing himself against the spotless transparent back wall, leaving sweat marks there, screaming at every perceived mishit, smashing racquets into the tiled floor, every point another opportunity to grasp perfection or failure. Anything short of perfection in others was unacceptable. He complained about the *fucking Fascist pedestrians* in this town, how they would dawdle across intersections and hold up traffic. *Drivers should clip a few of them, just to teach them*, he would snap, and then he leaned on his horn, *leaned* on it. This is where I made my stand, and I said, very quietly, *The day a pedestrian runs over a car driver, that's when you get to complain*. And that must have broken something in his head, because he just gaped at me, and shortly after that he told me he was getting off his Paxil, because it didn't make him feel right. *I want to be the real me again*. And I said to him: *But what if the real you is an asshole?* But it was too late, he had influenced me, or maybe more accurately, he reintroduced me to a part of myself, this habit of telling people what they should be doing, pushing and provoking, obsessing about *what next, what now*. I have always been one to intentionally overdo it, scrabble at greatness so hard that it eludes me, but at least I have my excuse: *I tried as hard as I could* ... I would attempt to learn guitar, but it would soon devolve into me slashing at the strings, gripping the fretboard like a lifeline, the tips of my fingers raw, my knuckles popped open, but I could feel good about my defeat, because I suffered for it, just as I suffered when I wrote the book. The guitar sits in the corner and my son tips it over with a musical *thunk*. The sound reminds me that all stringed instruments are the innards of animals, the true guts. I am strangling your guts. And for the first time since childhood, I say the words *Fuck me*, and it is such a needless, pleasurable release. *Fuck me*.

My father was murdered. After all he had been through, moving to another country, living another life with the hope of abandoning the previous one, he was snuffed out like it was nothing. Late day at the university, a thunderstorm at night, driving alone down Route 40, minding his own business, and then the screech, the full force of the 18-wheeler driving him against the railing, a chance ribbon of metal slamming through windshield, gashing his forehead. And yet, even then, his face a bloody wound and his right eye punctured like an olive, he still breathed, his body squirmed. But the trucker who collided with him was drunk, scared, playing scenarios in his head. Make it look like an accident. Push the car off the side of the road, off the cliff. It must have been a sight, the pot-bellied trucker and the shadow he cast, his boots tracking prints in the soaked granite, how he tore at his beard under a full moon as he considered the man slumped against the wheel, his remaining eye hidden under his disheveled hair, breathing, still breathing.

The headlights are like tracers, sighting and pinpointing the target. They come straight at me. Finally, the moment that was always incipient, anticipated, previewed in my head like a bad B-movie, and just as in the movie like a stupid animal I stare at the lights, even as the rest of me catches up and screams *Move move move!* And then shame, because the headlights are those of my own car, it was a trick of reflection, the chrome bumper of the truck in front of me, or the mirrored glass of the billboard this side of the rise. All around me, other cars rush. It is a pity. I was ready for the crash, and now I must cope with the pain in my ear that dominates my head, runs all the way down the back of my neck, straight to my heart like an injection. It is too much, it is always too much. I imagine it, that's what I am told, I am merely imagining my misery, isn't that what we are always told? *It's all in the head.* But why is that statement always tossed off, undervalued? When the bodies are gone and forgotten, it is all in the head, and that is the disgust of it all, it is all inside *me*, nowhere else. I pull off the side of the road, the gutter rattling underneath, plush leather seat stabbing me in the back, and even this is welcome as it diverts from the pain in head and heart, but not enough. *Just end it*, that's what I tell myself, but foolish me, commands do not exist. I reach into my purse, grab hold of the taser, and point it at myself. I breathe heavy, I must work up the courage every time, because all pain is remembered, even if these are mere fractions compared with what wracks my head. The taser's twin tips nuzzle my skin. I press the contact. Breath is trapped, my head is flung back and I am staring at the car's upholstered ceiling, my eyes are the only thing that move, everything else is locked, as if chains have been thrown around me and pulled. It is an interesting sensation, and I muse about it like a scientist, as an experiment is balanced on the edge between hope and fruition. And then the muscles contract, stretch, pull, breath dies in my throat, even the air is wrenched now. No good, I am still conscious. One more time. I am building an immunity to this, like I did with the pills. So once again, prods to skin, activate. There is a moment before I black out, and that moment is a tide, a blessing, feeling dribbling away from limbs, heart, mind, cracking and chipping off like paint, and I look at my sweaty face in the rear-view mirror. A pleasant sight, just like when I was a child and I admired myself after an entire afternoon of playing, and there was no injustice, no fear, no righteousness, because it was what it was. Sweat away your troubles, blood, sweat, and tears, and I hear Father now, calling for dinner. *Ready?* he shouts. *Ready* I shout back to him, confirmation and emulation, *Ready*.

The national army was approaching. News spread among the occupying soldiers that their comrades stationed at the next town down the river had been massacred. Not through some worthy stratagem—the soldiers were dying of thirst, and the only way to replenish their supply was to venture down to the riverbank. So the opposing army awaited them, and sure enough, the soldiers appeared, either alone or in small groups, scrambling or crawling, or even walking because they didn't care, they didn't think, their need was commanding them. And the opposing army took them down, just like a fairground gallery, *pop pop pop*. So now they were moving in, it would soon be over, and with war's conclusion would be trials, convictions, even a few executions. But even as the invading soldiers gathered in the central square, sat on their behinds in neat rows like good children, some of them openly weeping, awaiting orders that would never come, others were being dispatched to the far hills, the western mountains. The commander had only one directive for them: *Do not surrender. The war continues.* And with that task done, the commander retreated to his private chamber, festooned with the tapestries and skeletons and jade tables he had acquired in his conquests, and calmly disemboweled himself with a knife. Even as his blood ran in rivulets across the marble tiled floor, he allowed himself an instant's appreciation of the luxury around him, the worthiness of these captured cultural artifacts, and with a flutter of eyelashes, he expired at peace. The men he sent to the mountains were never heard from again, and many surmise that the wolves and bandits took care of them, even though there is no evidence either way. And so that particular war came to an end decades ago, the rubble and burned stalks of village buildings long since overrun by ring roads and skyscrapers and sewage drains that still stink of shit in the long hot summer months, and people still wear plain cotton shirts like they did fifty years before, even though their hair may be longer and they wear sunglasses that dazzle with reflected light. Yet somewhere in the mountains the remaining members of the commander's army may yet be hiding, their skin leathery with age, their hair white and as unruly as wire but their uniforms immaculate, still huddling around a fire at night, nibbling with deadened teeth at the remains of the wolf they killed the night before, still solemn and purposeful as they debate the next day's events, or the time when help will arrive, or the plan that will allow them to claim final victory. As the fire dies, they sing a song of the homeland, just a murmur, for it is not good to attract attention, and as they share lyrics and remind each other of the forgotten words, their wizened faces continue to burn with camaraderie.

My sister is in a good place today, so I drive her and my son out to the headlands, to a place of plentiful lakes and forest, just a little getaway. My son urges us both, *Come on, come on.* It will be our last time out together—I know this without knowing the particulars of the future, it is just that my mind is clear on this. *Come on, come on,* he still says. Doesn't he know that I only see the dead leaves that are pasted to the ground with mildew, or the bruises on my sister's bare legs? My sister and I are arguing about money. All the arguments are about money in the end. Very New Age. Even in this deathly beautiful place, we are quarreling. She smiles, as she always does to end our debates. It is as if she is saying, *You have nothing to compete with this.* I see those teeth stained brown, and I want to yell at her, *Can't you see?* And yet, her hair is cut short and pert, she wears a dress colorful as a daisy, and the smell of honeysuckle bathes her. I can lie to myself, and imagine that the odor emanates from deep within her, just this once. And still my son yells and encourages, and the trail leads deeper into the forest. He jogs ahead, cutting through the fog and mist. He has such confidence in his body and his whereabouts—it is a talent I never possessed. Like headlights at night, I can only see to the next bend in the curve, but beyond that is pure abyss. He is giggling, I hear his sneakers squeak against the ground, and this is good because it distracts me from my sister. Still, she is saying something that seems strangely significant: ...*Brutal honesty is just a form of selfishness,* she concludes. What was the beginning of that last thought? I missed it. She would say something like that, her and all that no-mind, heart-centered philosophy and tanned skin and perfume that drowns out her imperfections. My ear is buzzing, and I am resigned that it will never stop. I walk the trail that hugs hill and hollow, and the fresh winds pry me open, fill my head, freeze everything, like how the back of my mouth goes numb when I eat ice cream too fast. *Come on, come on,* my son urges, and finally I can laugh. I chase after my boy, my sister ambling behind. And then the path becomes something that could still be a path, or a random bunch of footprints on leaves. Maybe just mud that resembles a path. I am calling for my son to wait up, and even my sister is out of sight, left behind. Clouds muffle the sun, and each step leads me further into shade. It is as if I have stepped through a trap door. The temperature has dropped. The wind kicks up, the trees weave and sway. It is difficult to tell in the dimness, but there seems to be frost on the plants around me, caking the bushes. I blink hard, stop dead, perhaps I have taken a wrong turn, and in the moment I pause, I hear the approach of something, perhaps an animal. It is clear to me now: my son is running from this thing, and he is trying to lead me, in all my stupidity, to safety. Best to stand here, let whatever it is that follows us take me. To sacrifice myself would be noble. But just ahead, the sun breaks impossibly through the foliage. Shards of light fall on a madrone tree, a mammoth one, clinging to what appears to be solid stone, the base of it broad enough to cradle me if I choose to lie on it. Its dying branches spread out in intricate networks, branches sprouting from branches, like those matryoshka dolls which house smaller and smaller dolls. Each branch stretches in an uncharted direction, each indicating a distinct destiny. I hear my son call again, *Come on, come on*—he is far from me now—and my sister, equally far, in a different place, calling my name, the sound of it as bright and direct and heartbreaking as when we were young. And with that I remember, one day in the park, my father smiling at me with his washed-out, kindly face, my sister yelling all our names as she chased insects and smudged her knees with the green from the grass, my mother reading me stories of magical monkeys and demons, these tales always about journeys fraught with incidents, seemingly never-ending, and my mother's stomach would rise and fall with her breaths, as if she was instantly pregnant, back to normal, pregnant again, back and forth. Unable to move, I stare at this tree, the wind stopped, all sounds erased, even the steps of the unseen stranger, even the crashing surf of my headache. And then, ever so slowly, I can hear the ground pulse beneath me, thousands of heartbeats piled on top of each other, whispering:

When nothing is left of my body but ashes, even then, my love and hate will always burn.

National Holiday

THE LITTLE PRINCE WAS TOLD: WHENEVER *possible, stay in the room. A supervised tour of the local temple has been approved, dining out is no problem, but we advise you to stay in as much as you can during the weekend, especially on National Day.* The telephone and television had been removed, the hotel wi-fi deactivated. On the bedstand was a tiny electric tray upon which one could burn chemical wafers to keep the mosquitoes away. Although the Little Prince hadn't seen the device in years, just the sight of it reinstituted memories of its smothering, mentholated scent.

But why a room with *this* view of the golden slice of beach? Maybe just an attempt to pacify the journalist. He would be intoxicated by the view, and he would forget, just a little bit, why he was there and who was with him. But now the sand and ocean shimmied before them, taunting them, and the Little Prince would later blame his restlessness, and everything that happened afterwards, on the sight.

The empty beer can tumbled end over end past the Little Prince's head, hit the wall, and landed straight up on the bed, just for a moment, before tipping over in comical slow motion. *Another*, the journalist belched. They were both taking turns tossing cans, in a competition to see who would land his upright first. The journalist had opened the contest with a bottle, which of course had splintered on impact. From that point on only cans were allowed, and now they had the hang of it, lofting them like badminton players tossing up a serve. The journalist had just finished his third beer so he was ahead in number of attempts. They hadn't unboxed the whiskey the journalist had insisted the Little Prince purchase from the hotel gift shop—some Scottish name impossible to pronounce based on the spelling. The journalist wanted to save the whiskey for National Day, so local cheap beer for now. Local and cheap—that described this place to the dot.

Drink, drink! the journalist insisted. The man had a reputation with alcohol. The Little Prince had researched him, browsed his Twitter feed (deactivated) along with the relevant message boards. To the Central Committee, he was "problematic," and to his followers he was the Rock 'n' Roll Blogger. He had the aging rocker look down at least: gaunt like a college student, straggling hair, bristle eternal on his cheeks, skin the texture of sun-worn leather. Roaming through backwater towns and provinces on his BMW knock-off 250cc motorcycle, the journalist would infiltrate hovel and village office alike, ferreting out corresponding inequities or injustices. All it took was some casual conversations and beer. No matter the secrets you hoard in your heart, beer will always pull them out, like the bluntest set of tweezers in the world. Too blunt, by the Central Committee's standards. Rooting out corruption was supposed to happen according to a precise schedule, each infraction and its corrective announced simultaneously, all the better to emphasize the government's responsiveness. The journalist, of course, had no use for drawn-out schedules. Thus: irritant.

The Little Prince passed over the journalist's fourth can of beer. He was nursing only his second, but the journalist seemed to have lost track of where they were in their competition. The air conditioning was on full blast, with no way to turn it off, and the edges of the window panes and sills had been painted shut, as strong as glue. Accident or design? He didn't know. Like two mice under glass. When the Little Prince was a kid his father had dragged him to a local police station in the capital, not far from the main square, right behind a KFC and Starbucks. Inside, his father had herded him into a cell, and then slammed the door shut on him, just to make a point (the Little Prince had long forgotten what the point was—respecting the power of authority, or some such). For a good half hour the Little Prince sat alone, watching the dust play under the single light bulb high above, and it was almost pleasant listening to his own rapid breaths. When he and his father were driven home afterwards, he asked his father if he himself had been in a cell before, and his father had replied: *Someday I may be.*

The journalist hefted a fresh beer bottle in his hand; they had moved on to bottles now. *I could throw this at your head, knock you out, and escape.*

You could try. You wouldn't succeed.

Why did the hotel manager call you Little Prince?

My father used to live here. Big cadre back in the day.

You're a princeling, eh? That's a shame. I thought it might be a Saint-Exupéry reference.

Who?

Forget it. Western decadence. You can't understand.

The young man rolled his eyes. Not much in common. The journalist could have been a chimney, he smoked so much. Didn't act like anyone who had excelled at university, either. Still, his most galling attribute was his smell. Earlier, when the Little Prince had examined the man's luggage as a matter of routine, he had discovered threadbare flannel shirts, one pair of jeans, a few sets of soiled underwear, and nothing that resembled deodorant. Now a smell like rotten eggs was thick in the air—either the man had farted or this was his natural musk. His bare feet were stuffed into the flimsy white cloth slippers the hotel had provided. More stink.

Would you like to take a shower? the Little Prince asked.

The journalist's lips were clamped on the mouth of his bottle. He regarded the Little Prince with something close to a cross-eyed look. He finished his swig, burped loudly. *No*, he said.

What could be done? It wasn't as if the Little Prince could ask his superiors for permission to forcibly wash the journalist. He was supposed to report in after the National Holiday, and not a day before. Any earlier contact meant an emergency, thus failure. Everyone else back at the capital would be busy at parades, waving flags, maybe enjoying an immortal second or two on national TV. This little sojourn with the journalist was intended to be circumspect, and forgotten out of existence almost immediately. It was why they had picked this comatose seaside town, far out of season.

You know this town well? the journalist asked. He was staring out the window at the beach, the tufted waves.

Not really. My father grew up here, but my family moved to the capital before I was born.

Became a bigwig and cashed in, eh? Congratulate him for

me.

He's in the hospital. In no condition to receive congratulations.

Really? What happened?

With an effort, the Little Prince said, *If you're hungry, we can order room service.*

Another *bang* as the journalist tossed his bottle at the wall. This time it was a hard throw, and the bottle made it to the bed in two uneven pieces.

You're disqualified, the Little Prince said. His face was wet. Blood? Splinter from the bottle? No, just cheap beer.

I passed through here years ago, the journalist said. *Just after it became a vacation getaway for Great Leaders. Back when all these Soviet-style hotels were new, but they looked old and beat-up even then. And I've met people older than me who remember when this whole place was all coastal forest. That's when you realize you're just an insignificant link in this gigantic chain…*

The Little Prince screwed his eyes shut, hoping that the taste of beer would eradicate the journalist's smell, or at least dull his ears to the man's lecture. It didn't matter whose side you were on—it always came down to lectures. A lot of talk, and what had it gotten the journalist? Labels like "disruptive" and "unpatriotic," years wasted in house detention and prison. And each time, the journalist would be taken aback by the official response. Such a spectacular lack of understanding about how the world worked. Like a child expecting a different reaction from his parents every time he threw his food on the floor.

Once you take away all the trees, that's when the wind comes in. Stirring up all the loose dust. Erosion. I've seen it happen in the interior. The local authorities don't care about that. We won't be around when there's nothing left but shit, so who cares, right? Funny thing is, just a few weeks ago...

The Little Prince had emphasized the rules during arrival: *We have a decent budget for food, and can eat out anytime. There will be no demands on you during your stay, no struggle sessions. In return, no using other people's phones or computers or tablets, no posting of any content. Absolutely no political discussions with strangers.* Both men knew the journalist was well within parameters by gabbing away like this in private, and the journalist didn't give a damn if the Little Prince reported the subject matter—it was nothing he hadn't posted before.

I visited a factory town once in the central provinces, the journalist went on. *They burned coal day and night. When I arrived the sky was black, truly black. Never seen anything like it. So much soot in the air that the moon was red as blood. The people who lived there were black ghosts. Two eyes, white as diamonds, the rest of them black. Black on the outside and on the inside. In the lungs, in the belly. I bribed someone to check the death registries. Do you know, life expectancy in that region is...*

The man really needed a shower. The Little Prince could force him. He could assume responsibility for that unilateral decision. If the journalist became uncooperative, he could call in the third member of their group, the moon-faced comrade stationed outside the door. They could turn on the water full blast, pin the journalist, and they'd all get soaked, which wasn't such a bad idea on a day like this. Still, there would be a lot of fuss, and the young man wanted to avoid his colleague as much as possible, since he liked him even less than the journalist. Clearly the man was from the sticks, with that vacant stubborn look on his face so many had out there. The Little Prince knew that if he ever fell from favor, he would be under the heel of men just like him. He would be dispatched to a remote region where the summers were brutal and the autumn would last a week or two at the most before winter crashed in. He would shovel manure, or lay scalding blacktop, and the local peasants would be his supervisors. They would stand off to the side, smoking and laughing at him, cajoling and denying, and every once in a while granting, if in the proper mood. It was the unique privilege of intellectuals to be subservient to the peasants in the end. Naturally his colleague and the journalist got on just fine, trading cigarettes as if they were old buddies. The Little Prince didn't smoke himself, not after what he saw it do to his father.

Aloud, the Little Prince said: *If you talked like this in the old days, you would be blindfolded, and hot cooking oil would be poured down your ears.*

The journalist laughed. *Who says that hasn't happened?*

Let's not pretend, the Little Prince said. *You don't want to be here and I don't want to be here, smelling your stink. If we go out for a drink, will you stop with the black lungs and deforestation?*

The journalist didn't answer, but his feet were already back in his lumpy black boots. Within a few minutes they were seated on the emptied-out hotel veranda, just above the beach, baking in the heat. It had to be some kind of temperature record—this time of year was notorious for fog and drizzle. Just further torture. Who wanted to be stuck alongside this stinky journalist on a day like this, when the cool blue water was a mere minute in front of them? Even the Little Prince's colleague had the benefit of being stationed a few tables away. Fine, let him stay away. His impassive act was wearisome. It would have been better if the man was hostile, obsequious, anything. The Little Prince let his gaze wander over to the backsides of the other hotels, most of them closed for good, mottled by mildew. At the town's peak a decade or two before, the bustle would have stretched down the beach for miles.

The hotel manager approached, and once again the *How are you, Little Prince?* Hot tea was poured—why did this country insist on drinking hot tea in hot weather, the Little Prince wondered—and menus in wrinkled laminate were passed around.

Popular here, aren't you Little Prince? the journalist said.

Came here a few times when I was a kid, the Little Prince answered. He was just old enough to know that one tends to romanticize youth, but the place really had gone to shit. Same tablecloths as years before, blanched by the sun. Cobwebs upon cobwebs clumped in the corner of the awning, like tiny cities that had disintegrated before achieving critical mass. Off to the side, in the shade, a fox terrier was collapsed on his side. The animal was panting with the ferocity of a choo-choo train. *You and me both*, the Little Prince thought. The hotel manager usually locked the dog in a wire-mesh cage only a few feet high, so being allowed to lounge around, even in this heat, must have been a luxury. More than anything, the Little Prince wanted to find a scooter and buzz around the bend of the shore to the windward side. A nice secluded restaurant somewhere, Christmas lights for decoration, local eats: fried rice, diced ham, miniature shrimp, green onions, eggs cooked halfway between scrambled and over easy. Here the hotel menu was tourist-centric: hamburger (he grimaced at the thought of a patty burned to black, a bun on the verge of collapse) and pizza (he didn't even want to think how that would look).

Look at all that... the journalist was staring across the broad expanse of beach, out to sea. *The time it takes to walk down there, you might run into two people*, he murmured.

Walk the same distance in the city, and you'll bump into hundreds, thousands. Just shows there's a long way to go. So much more we could fuck up.

The Little Prince cleared his throat.

You seem awfully young to be "traveling," the journalist pressed on. *They run out of bodyguards?*

No, they just deemed you less important than the other activists. The Little Prince was happy to get in that little jab, at least.

I'm honored. You've done this before? Any dissidents try to escape on your watch?

No political discussion. That was the deal.

Just asking. Not like I'm going to write about this.

I know you aren't.

You know the original Greek root of the word "politics" is basically "citizen"? We're simply two citizens, talking.

I know, because "We all have an obligation as citizens to ask questions." I've read your blog. Does your wife ask you questions about your mistress?

Ha! Now you're talking politics. What's he thinking about, I wonder?

What? The Little Prince followed the journalist's gaze over to the other minder. The man had lounged back in his chair, ankle crossed over knee, shirt unbuttoned to mid-chest, affecting an air of indifference. Yet his face was drenched in sweat.

My theory is that he's observing you, not me, said the journalist. *He's going to report on your performance.*

If that's true, then maybe you can make a run for it. It'll look good when I have you on the ground, with your arm broken.

The journalist laughed, a great stinky laugh, and for the first time the Little Prince noticed that his incisors were as sharp as fangs. *Fuck it! I like you, even if you don't want me to.*

The manager returned with complimentary cheap beers. The journalist wanted something called "sex on the beach," and the manager threw up his hands in apology, completely uncomprehending. He did snicker at the name of the drink, though.

How is your father? the manager asked the Little Prince. The man's jaws were working on gum, smacking up and down, seized with nervousness or excess energy. *Haven't seen him for a while. Tell him to come back. We'll make sure we have a banquet ready. On the house, naturally.*

The Little Prince couldn't look at the man. He didn't deserve this deference. Was his father truly the manager's old buddy, or was the manager just presenting this face to the son of the powerful official? This was the basic stratagem for living: Be nice to those who you can't afford not to be nice to. And what would the manager say if he told him about the current state of the powerful official who was his father?

The Little Prince asked him: *Is your niece around?*

The manager sighed. *A sad story. Who knows where she is these days? She was always a little crazy, you know.* With a final significant look, as if acknowledging that certain things should not even be uttered, he departed.

The journalist regarded the Little Prince with awakening interest. *What's that all about?*

Old friend, the Little Prince said. Just being on the veranda was bringing back memories. She would sit across the table from him, both their legs too short to reach the ground. She was too thin back when they first met, and she would only grow thinner as she grew taller. Her eyes, though, were big, too big for the rest of her. They had an unreal gleam to them. He kept forgetting her name, so he just called her Little Niece to her face, or Summer Girl inside his head. He was never able to stop staring at the mole at the tip of her nose. Rather than sitting flush with the skin, it rose like a little bulb. Surely she knew how prominent it was. Why didn't she ever have it removed?

Tell me about her, the journalist pressed on.

Nothing to tell.

Is she the one who's been sending you texts all day? Don't think I haven't noticed.

That's someone in the capital.

Playing the field, eh? A girl in each town?

That's your technique.

Tell me about the one in the capital, then.

She likes to think I'm her boyfriend.

Oh, aren't we confident.

The Little Prince snorted. *Not me. She sends me bunches of photos from her day. She works at the Convention Center. Same shit all the time. Female presenters in bikinis—*

—With no hips, I bet, the journalist interjected.

—and men in dark suits and greased hair.

The standard Party look? Hair dyed black, everyone wearing the same dark suits?

No sense of style, the Little Prince muttered. *You'd think they'd loosen up a bit. And don't even think about telling people I said that, because I'll deny it.*

Very careful, aren't you?

And the aggravating thing is, her photos are always blurry. She doesn't know how to take photos but she takes them all the time.

So teach her.

She's not my type. We'll go to a movie, or the theater, and there's a video she'll want to see, and she'll play it right there on her phone, in the middle of a show, full volume. Just obnoxious.

Like a lot of people in this country these days.

You're above all that, are you?

I didn't mean that.

So what does your mother do?

She died when I was young.

What's your father up to these days?

How about you shut up, and we'll go for a walk.

The three of them made their way down to the sand, the Little Prince's colleague maintaining his distance behind them. The Little Prince could imagine that he and the journalist were important Mafia dons in a Hollywood movie, replete with entourage of trailing bodyguards. The Little Prince's slacks were dark, polyester, and now stuck to his legs with sweat. *Just as stylish as our great leaders,* he thought. Beyond the abandoned hotels and a thicket of tallow trees at the far end of the beach, music was playing, too distant to discern melody or language. Without thinking or discussing it, they headed in that direction. It was that magic time of day in which the light glancing off the waves was brighter than the sun in the sky. The Little Prince was reminded of when he was a kid, splashing in the water, sand under his toenails and salt in his eyes. His father would tow him along, his middle three fingers easily grabbing his tiny hand.

You're a tough one to figure out, said the journalist. *You're clearly not a regular official. They're way more formal. Plus they'd take full advantage of that expense account and get us a few seafood banquets. You're a princeling but you haven't taken the bait on my little rants, and you don't seem so corrupted. So who are you?*

I'm just trying to do my job.

Spoken like a true proletariat. Or opportunist.

They were leaving the main stretch of hotels behind.

Beyond the drooping trees, the beach was laced with random shards of stone and splayed-out seaweed. On a rise just above the sand, a row of small open-air bars fanned out. The structures had been fishing shacks in their previous lives, but cherrywood had replaced particle boards, fish hooks had been stripped out for drink cabinets, and neon signs had been planted. The Little Prince remembered these bars from his summer vacations. Each establishment would blare music through muscled-up DJ speakers. It was a carnival and competition—which bar would overcome through sheer volume? Move a few meters and the ballad of a local chanteuse would sharpen into a Western disco tune.

This evening, the beach was empty, and all the shacks chained and boarded up, save for one. It didn't even have a name; the only thing that differentiated it from the others was the coat of red paint on the barn-like doors, which had been pulled wide open. The song was originating from inside: Captain and Tennille's "Love Will Keep Us Together."

The Little Prince couldn't help smiling—he knew this particular bar well. He had always had a weakness for it because of the jukebox. Either by design or malfunction, the jukebox could only play three songs. His father would bring him here whenever he had dealings with the local officials, and it would always be an event he could brag about back at school: *I'm the only kid they ever allowed in this bar!* While the Little Prince's father gabbed away over beers (alcohol, the keystone of any successful deal), he would stand sentry at the jukebox, staring at the song selections as they flipped back and forth on their tiny steel hinges.

As they arrived, the solitary woman tending the bar counter didn't give the journalist a second look. Of course no one out here would be familiar with him, reasoned the Little Prince. In this town no one gave a shit about the plight of coal miners, or why the water supply of a small mountain town in a different province where locals spoke an unrecognizable dialect might be getting poisoned. No one cared because there were already enough things that needed to be gotten on with, and one would simply go crazy if one thought about an entire nation's problems.

Sex on the beach for everyone! the journalist belted out, slapping the counter like a sailor fresh off a year-long cruise.

Got it, the woman said. She pulled out three mini-bottles of vodka, like those found in a hotel room minibar.

What's your name? the journalist asked. *Wait. No real names. What's your English name? Do you have one?*

Yes. Maddie.

Oh. He sighed. *That's bad. I used to know a woman with that name. I hated her. That means you'll have to work extra hard to impress me.* He said this very solemnly, as if it was a sacred task not for the faint of heart.

Okay.

You don't have a guitar, do you, Maddie?

Nope, sorry. She drew out the word *sorry* so it became a drawl, an invitation.

That's too fucking bad. I'm pretty good. At least, better than this guy over here. He winked at the Little Prince. *Young people, they only do karaoke these days. Me, I can play three chords and the truth.*

The truth about what?

Me. How old do you think I am?

She gave him a look, a quick one. *Sixty?*

You flatterer! Fifty next month. I hope I don't make it to sixty. The older you get, the more mistakes you make.

You must be making a lot of mistakes, then.

He laughed—again the fangs came out—and she joined in.

When you reach the point where your mistakes outnumber the things you get right, what's the use of living? Don't answer. Hey, Little Prince, say something. You nervous being around this lovely girl?

"*Little Prince*"? She laughed. *Is he right, Little Prince?*

You're a silly old man, the Little Prince said to the journalist. The words just came out, without hesitation or thought.

The journalist beckoned for fresh shots, and Maddie obliged. *I'm silly, and you're the one paying for the drinks*, he said. *But you see, Maddie? He was too shy to tell you. The indecision of youth. Me, I can say that I do exactly what I wanted to do. And for the next five years, that will include hanging out with you.*

Five years with you might be a bit long, she said.

The Little Prince guessed she was about his age. She wore her hair in a simple ponytail, like all the young girls in propaganda posters, the non-city girls. She had the untouched, freckled, natural appearance most women in small towns have before the hard life takes hold, before the premature wrinkles and age spots. An aquamarine tank top hung loose on her shoulders. No breasts to speak of, but he didn't mind that. So much anxiety about how local women's breasts couldn't compete with those in other countries, but then they wouldn't have to worry about old age, and boobs hanging down to their stomachs.

You're right, the journalist said. *A couple of days of me would be enough. What song next? Got any Sade?*

Who?

Sade. "Smooth Operator." If you ask me what sex sounds like, I would say it sounds like her voice.

Oh, she said.

This jukebox plays only three songs, the Little Prince said. *Captain and Tennille, John Denver—*

Okay! No one move. Another round, Maddie, shots this time. Any liquor you like. I'll take care of the jukebox.

A fresh set of glasses was deployed before the Little Prince. In the fading light the drinks had a licorice hue. To black livers, the Little Prince thought, and threw back the drink.

So you've been here before, Maddie said to him.

Been a while. Is the cat still around?

Which cat? A lot of them wander through.

It was a tuxedo. I think her name was Panda. About that big. Kind of had the face of a martial arts master. Shed her fur a lot. The last time I was here she was seven years old.

When was that?

Seven years ago. He thought: Was that cat here? Or some other bar? Maybe it was somewhere else. He didn't care. He just wanted to talk to her.

That's a while. What kept you away?

I live in the capital now. He knew it sounded boastful as soon as he said it, so he added a little shrug, as if to say, *No big deal.*

Nice. She was smiling now. Or at least she seemed to. Jägermeister—that was what the Little Prince had just drank. He knew it from his days over at Embassy row, hanging out with all those foreign students and tourists. He was loath to move his head, or shift his eyes. Right now they were resting on the bar woman's bare shoulder.

You been there? he asked.

The shoulder shrugged. *Vacation. It was okay. I was alone, and it's better to travel with friends.*

Well, you have one now.

Uh-huh, she laughed. She put out a plate of halved bananas. *No, I don't know any cats named Panda. She probably died a while ago.*

Or she moved on. Sought out new territory to conquer.

Founded a new nation, she agreed.

Sired hundreds of citizens already. Starting anew. The younger generation always improves on the old.

And thank Heaven for that, the journalist cut in, sweeping up his shot glass. *Old people always fuck things up. I can't get the jukebox started.*

If you selected the song, it'll start in a minute, the Little Prince said. *It takes its time.*

They were all at the bar now, partaking of the bananas. They ate in silence, the peels wilting on the plate, the air soon fragrant with banana breath. The journalist and the Little Prince's colleague were sharing cigarettes again, and the Little Prince didn't care. He didn't even mind the mosquitos buzzing about their drinks—they were just trying to enjoy their sliver of time before the night breeze blew in. John Denver was on, and they all mouthed the lyrics silently, for somehow it was one of those songs that everyone seemed to know. Then the song hit the first chorus, and as if it had been pre-planned, they were all singing out loud, even the Little Prince's colleague. The journalist had badly accented English (that was to be expected, the older generation didn't have foreign teachers back then), but he gamely kept up as they all warbled about mountain mamas in West Virginia.

The Little Prince was looking at Maddie. She was drumming her fingers on the bar in an improvised counter-rhythm. He wanted to see under her tanktop. Meanwhile, the journalist had crossed the line between melody and shouting. It was all okay; they were all a little drunk and a little goofy. And then, just as quickly as this pleasant realization had dawned on them, the song ended. They all sat speechless, staring in different directions, allowing the chattering of the cicadas to fill the lull. The Little Prince blinked lazily. The buzz from the alcohol was radiating through his head in waves.

Somehow they ended up on folding beach chairs. A handful of them had been spread out in front of the bar, on the sand, facing the ocean. Like everything else, they were unraveling a bit. It was difficult to know how much time had passed, and the Little Prince was feeling too languid and satisfied to check the time on his phone, which was buried deep in his slacks, away from prying fingers. Captain and Tennille were on again, and the red sun hung just over the water now, about the length of a thumb above the waves. Next to him was the journalist, holding his empty shot glass, a couple of spent cigarette butts planted there. Miracle of miracles, the man didn't stink any more—the Little Prince could only smell the salt of the sea. The other minder was over by some bushes, his back to them. By the way he was crouched, his hands in front of him, it was clear he was taking a piss. Typical provincial, thought the Little Prince.

Arise, arise! the journalist sang tunelessly. Was he about to sing the national march? Then he coughed. *I mean, Sink! Sink!* He threw his hands towards the sun, as if making an offering.

The bar woman had emerged with some freshly cooked green onion pancakes. For the first time the Little Prince had a view of her legs; they were thinner than her arms. The pancakes had been cooked with eggs, the eggs fried over easy first before being tucked inside the dough.

Disregarding decorum, seized with hunger, they each grabbed a pancake. Soon their fingers were itchy with grease. Napkins were in short supply so they rubbed their hands against the fabric of their chairs, bringing them to a shine. Still tipsy, the Little Prince held back from speaking while the journalist and the bar woman bantered. Where was she originally from? *A small town the next province over.* Why was she here? *Just someplace to be for the summer.* But summer was over. Maybe she would stay for the winter too, as she was in no hurry to get home. But how did he know she wasn't a local? It was something in her eyes, something that indicated that this was all new to her. The journalist explained: *Nothing is more inspiring than seeing someone excited about life.*

You think? She frowned. *But it's only temporary. Soon I'll have to move on, and find another place that excites me.*

It's tough, isn't it? We all want to find the right place, so we can be... permanent. But nowhere is completely right, so eventually you settle for something less.

Inspiring words, said the Little Prince.

Ignoring him, the journalist said: *Ever go to an author reading? When an author talks about his book before he reads it, and you get excited by the author's passion... and then the author starts reading, and the book turns out to be pretty bad?*

Yes.

That's what living in this country feels like.

What's that? interrupted the Little Prince. He pointed down towards the water. From their vantage point, higher up on the beach, it looked like a charming little tiled roof, but that seemed unlikely, given the object's proximity to the ocean.

Want to see? Maddie had a look in her eyes, and the Little Prince thought: *Yes, there it is.*

She swung the doors of the bar shut, locking in Captain and Tennille, and led them towards the unidentified object.

She toted an LED lamp inside the papery confines of a traditional red lantern, fat and balloon-like, as if yearning to float skyward.

Do you look like your father? the journalist asked the Little Prince.

Why do you want to know? The Little Prince was annoyed anew. It was uncanny how the man could bring up stuff he didn't want to talk about.

They say that when a child is born, he looks like his father. It's a natural survival adaptation. A father is less likely to abandon a baby if it looks like him. But then as you grow, you can start looking more like your mother, or somebody else. Almost like you're choosing to be who you want to be. So who do you look like now?

I liked you better when you were singing badly.

In response, the journalist burped. The Little Prince burped a moment later. Soon they were in a belching contest, the journalist rearing up like a giant beast when it was his turn, marshalling the sound in his chest before unleashing. As they came closer to the water, the surf all but overwhelmed the burping, so they ceased.

What had looked like a roof was the top of a house boat. It was a boxy affair built to accommodate eight to ten people, and manifestly incapable of handling the ocean, even in ideal working condition. It was pointed optimistically towards the ocean, and that was as far as it had ever gotten. Now it was entrenched in the soggy sand a good distance from the water, listing permanently. Someone had hung an oak board over the windows on one side, perhaps for a sign that had never been painted. If there had been glass in the windows, it was long gone, and the slice of hull above the sand had ripened with rust.

Did somebody think they were going to be able to take this thing to sea? the Little Prince said.

Maybe some rich idiot, the woman replied. *Or they wanted to turn it into another bar.* She had brought a bottle of red wine—cheap, French, and good. They kicked off their shoes and settled down on the sand to pass the bottle around, leaning back against the side of the boat. The Little Prince laid himself on his side, opposite the journalist and Maddie. The sand was sticky against his arms, but it felt good to sink into it. As usual, the Little Prince's colleague was content to keep his distance. He squatted at the edge of the water, his shoes still on, and every so often a pure white cloud of cigarette smoke escaped him.

The journalist and Maddie were side by side, both their legs stretched out. In the lantern light, they looked closer in age, like brother and sister. The journalist gave her knee a little poke with his, and she poked back. *So why are you here?* he asked her. *I ask a lot of questions, you see. It's my job.*

Will this be published somewhere?

Nope. Because I'm terrible at my job. Or at least, terrible at being published. But I'm hungry for people's stories.

She took a deep breath, than shrugged. *Got nowhere else to be. No family. I just move from place to place.*

Where's your family?

Father left me and my mom at an early age. Then my mom went a little crazy. She didn't have any jobs, any friends or family who could help. Zero prospects. So she tried to kill me.

The journalist placed his hand on her shoulder. *Damn you,* thought the Little Prince.

She took me out to the woods, Maddie continued, *and she tried to slash my wrists. I think her idea was that she would kill me, then kill herself. I was five years old, but I had a sense of what was happening. So I broke away and ran. The police took my mom in after that. For a while I stayed with my aunt. She was nice, but I hated being there. One of those places where every healthy person goes to the South to work in the factories the whole year, and they only come home for Spring Festival. The rest of us, the old people and kids, stay at home and farm all day, for barely any money. What I remember about living there is everyone coming home for the festival, a couple of weeks of banquets and laughing, and then back to sadness and hunger the other 50 weeks of the year. So I left. Seen so many towns, I can't count them.*

She let out another *Hmm*, not on the verge of another thought so much as punctuating the end of the story.

Thanks for telling me that, said the journalist.

You've heard stories like that before? she said.

Similar ones. I've been around a lot too. And I'm being serious here, I have great respect for you. I believe that travelers know more than other people. You will forever be wiser than everyone else your age.

It's nice to think so, she said.

Her head was at a quizzical angle as she leaned back against the hull. The Little Prince thought of the ancient marble vessel at the old Summer Palace in the capital, forever moored in the lake. This ship was nowhere near as grand, and yet both were beached, both had never experienced ocean, and both were smothered in melancholy. He thought: *Even empress dowagers and millionaires disappear, but they leave their clutter in their wake, reminding us that they were here.* Maddie, with her hair down over her shoulder like that, resembled a portrait of a woman sitting by a frosted window, or looking out from a pagoda somewhere amongst surging mountains, awaiting someone's return.

She passed the wine bottle back to the journalist. *Are you married?* she asked him.

He took a short, confident swig. *Yes.*

But no wedding ring.

My wife and I have an arrangement. We don't see each other too often, anyway.

Doesn't sound very easy.

Ask him about his mistress, the Little Prince said. He hated bringing it up the moment he said it, but he was in an ornery mood all of a sudden.

Mistress?

Sure, I've got one up the coast. He struck up a cigarette. *She has a boy. I support both of them.*

Your kid?

Yes. At least, she tells me he's mine. Guess I never thought to confirm it.

Or you just didn't care.

Sure. It's fair to say that, even if it's not true.

One of my friends married early, she said. *He and his wife can't stand each other. Arguing with each other day and night. I asked him why he didn't do anything about it. He said, Because it's just easier not to deal with it.*

Fuck... The journalist hacked up some smoke. *Fuck that. That's what happens when you don't know how to get what you want. You go insane.*

What does your wife want? asked the Little Prince.

I said, we have an arrangement. I don't worry about her, she doesn't worry about me. We're okay with it.

Again she made the *hmmm* sound—this time it sounded like a query. *I don't know if you're being mature or inhuman.*

The journalist laughed. *My brain's got limited capacity. I can only worry about so many things.*

I feel like a swim, Maddie said. *Anyone want to join?*

I can't swim, said the journalist. *I get seasick too. I'm more of a mountain man.*

Oh yes? she said, her eyes teasing. *Too bad.*

I'll just relax a bit, and watch you.

Me too, said the Little Prince. *I mean, I have to watch him. Make sure he stays out of trouble.*

She said *Hmmm* again. This time it was sardonic. She handed him the lantern and trotted off towards the edge of the shore. For a few moments the Little Prince could see her long limbs as they swayed forward; then she hopped into the water, and within seconds she was beyond the lantern's diameter of light.

Loving that girl is easy acapella, said the journalist, in English.

Huh?

Just a Sade song.

Do you think your Western influences make you cool?

No. I do think about Miles Davis a lot, though.

The trumpet guy?

That and much more, but the specifics aren't important. The point is, he brought up a lot of young musicians. Coltrane, Herbie Hancock, Tony Williams. He started a legacy, he got other people involved. I like that idea.

You better be careful, said the Little Prince. *With talk like that, you might get accused of fomenting dissent.*

Is that what you think I'm doing?

Fuck! The Little Prince yelled. The accumulated alcohol had done its work, and he needed to shout just to shout, because his body was so antsy. *Who gives a fuck what I think? Have some common sense. How do you think it looks to the Central Committee? I try to give you some fucking advice for once and you pull your interviewer crap. You ever think through the consequences of what you do?*

The journalist laughed. *This isn't a conversation for sober folks. Have more wine.*

I've already had enough. And you're not going to get me to drink so much that I'll say something I'll regret.

Shit, is being careful the hallmark of your generation or what? Sit through too many self-criticism sessions? All you think about is what you're not supposed to say.

It's called being smart. You should try it.

You know what you make me think of? A stone skipping across the water. You'll keep going for a while, you might think you're getting somewhere, but soon you'll disappear for good.

I could say the same for you.

With matching grunts they hauled themselves up. They strolled around to the port side, wine spilling after them like liquid crumbs. Just ahead of the houseboat, a canary-yellow inflatable dinghy lay dormant, tethered to the boat's prow. To the Little Prince, the sight of the small craft hooked up in such a manner, as if it was expected to drag the boat out to sea, was pitiful. The journalist staggered up the abbreviated stairs in the side of the houseboat to the deck, and the Little Prince followed with nary a hitch in his step (*Score one for my generation*, he thought). The cabin was all long shadows and floorboards that crackled underfoot. Save for two benches along each wall, it had been divested of all furnishings. There was a strong odor of something that might have been alive once—probably fish. To the Little Prince, it was preferable to the journalist's scent. The journalist sank down flat on one of the benches with a groan, and soon cigarette smoke was spiraling away from him towards the ceiling, like a cyclone in slow motion. The Little Prince sat upright on the opposite bench, the lantern at his side, casting reaper-like shadows all around.

Maybe we should go back to the hotel, he said.

You wouldn't want that, said the journalist. *I'm a very*

bad snorer. You wouldn't be able to sleep for one minute. I talk in my sleep too.

Better and better. Your wife must love that.

One time I was dreaming about being surrounded by spiders. I've seen a lot of spiders in my time. So I started shouting in my sleep: Spiders everywhere! They're on the walls! The floor! Scared the piss out of my wife. She just ran out of the bedroom screaming murder.

I would have done exactly the same. I fucking hate spiders.

Ha! I can imagine you running out of the room, too.

They both had an honest chuckle at that one. The journalist took in another gulp of wine, and gargled it.

The Little Prince asked: *What did you mean, you've seen a lot of spiders?*

In prison, said the journalist.

Oh.

I actually don't mind spiders too much. Rats, on the other hand... I had to raid a rat's nest for food once... but for some reason I don't dream about them. We don't have to talk about it.

I wasn't going to ask.

Not much to tell, anyway. I was one of the lucky ones. Just got a taste of the "reform through labor" bit. The bad part lasted only about two months for me. I didn't have to inform on anyone for favors, I didn't end up with a broken back or anything chronic. Not that it was easy. To be starving, really starving, ready to eat anything that isn't bolted to the floor—I wouldn't recommend it.

And yet you keep getting yourself into trouble.

I don't think about consequences—you said it. I think about the future. A hundred years ago our ancestors were shoveling manure. Now here we are today, drinking sex on the beach. Because the future tends to be better than the past. And the only reason this is true is because people work at making it so. They fucking slave at it.

Or maybe it doesn't matter, said the Little Prince. *You can stir things up as much as you want, but all these things you go to prison for will be gone and forgotten someday, and not due to any action you take. With or without us, the world goes on.*

Ha! That is some dark shit, young man. Or else it's the most idealistic thing I've ever heard. So it doesn't matter what we do, because we're destined to keep moving forward?

I mean... The Little Prince's words were starting to slur, and he knew it. *I'm not talking about karma or religion or even politics. But—forget it.*

Look at that. The journalist pointed his finger straight up, towards the heavens. The Little Prince was confused for an instant, but then he saw that he was indicating the porthole, and the moon sliding into view on the other side.

Reminds me of the poem— the Little Prince began.

With the sing-song, smart-aleck attitude of a grade school student, the journalist recited:

The moon outside the window
Lighting the ground
Resembles a touch of frost.

Feh! he grunted. *Why do we spend so much time memorizing rote stuff? Classical poetry, ballroom dance patterns, English vocabulary words for the GRE. No wonder we're in the rut we're in. Give me jazz every time.*

We all have to start somewhere. A common base, so we can relate to each other.

Boring. Like this talk is getting boring.

And yet I bet you can recite what went down in the International Hotel Conference fifty years ago, just before the revolution. You harp on the mistakes, and you dismiss the stuff that's made us great.

Great? Today the emperors have chauffeured rides in Buicks. That's what qualifies as great these days.

You can't enjoy anything for long, can you? Do you know how fucking lucky you are that I even let you come out and drink this much? Can you appreciate even one moment?

You go ahead and appreciate it. This time next week, I'll be in another moment. No relation whatsoever to this one.

Fuck. The Little Prince rubbed at his forehead. *I'm not going to let you make a move on Maddie.*

Ha! Is that where your mind's at? He drummed his heels lightly on the top of the bench, like a little kid. *I'm way too drunk to even think of getting it up right now. What about you? You making a move?*

The Little Prince didn't answer. He wrestled the wine bottle away from the journalist's soft grip and took a swig.

Or maybe you'll go looking for that hotel manager's niece? I want to hear more of that story.

The Little Prince stood, scuffled to the front of the boat, the vessel's acute angle a match for the wooziness in his head. With the lantern left behind in the cabin, his eyes were forced to adjust to the stars and the silvery waves. He could see a limb break the surface of the becalmed waters, disappear, then reappear. Maddie was being safe— it couldn't be more than a couple meters deep where she was. The mosquitos were gone and the landward breeze was tumbling forward, right in his face.

It had been seven summers since the Little Prince had been in the ocean. The Little Niece had insisted, *I feel like a swim.* Not that he needed much convincing—doing anything else on that blistering day was unthinkable. So they were both in the water, the sun glaring at them, and she was up against him, very deliberately so, so close that he could see the tiny tufts of hair under her armpits. He was taken aback a bit at the sight—girls in the city shaved from an early age—but he knew that girls like the Little Niece weren't exposed to much style or fashion. They splashed around a while in the dead heat, and soon she had her arms around him and her head on his shoulder. He was just standing there in the water, and her head was next to his, as she stood tippy-toe on his feet and shins, both of them close to floating away, her big eyes not daring to look into his. So he ended all suspense and kissed her, not through any sense of love or chivalry, but only because he felt that if he didn't, then what was supposed to happen next wouldn't happen at all.

The journalist was snoring. The man hadn't lied—he snored like a motherfucker. Distractedly, the Little Prince dipped his hand inside his pants and stroked his penis. Sex with the Little Niece had been disappointing. Of course he didn't know it then, it had all been a new experience for him, but looking back on it, it was not a good fit. There are people you are compatible with on an emotional or intellectual level, but when you're having sex, it can boil down to how well a curve in the other person's body matches a hollow in your own body. The Little Niece had been all knobby knees and elbows. She gasped throughout, as if she was hyperventilating. It was like trying to pin down an animal. No doubt he had been similarly disappointing to her, but afterwards she laid her head on his chest and kept saying *Thank you*, over and over. He had the impression she wasn't thanking him for the sex, but for everything else.

As he continued masturbating, he thought of Maddie. Her legs really were the legs of a model. Perhaps that was too extreme to say. Models had legs like twigs. Just another symptom of Westernization. His girl back at the capital aspired to have thin legs. She had tried all kinds of cleansing diets and toning exercises. It was no use for her, her ankles were just too thick. It wouldn't look good. Shut up, he told himself. He was losing his erection. Back to the bar woman. She was from the countryside. They would be up for anything. No preconceptions or inhibitions. Good lips too. He could imagine them whispering in his ear. All he had to think about were specific body parts. The length of an arm. Fingers plucking at his chest.

Hey! someone called, from outside the boat. *Hey!*

The Little Prince turned. The cabin was empty. His colleague was the one who had shouted; he was staggering into view, pointing out at the ocean. *There!* he said.

The dinghy had glided out to meet Maddie, and the journalist was laid out flat on it, stomach down, peering over the side, as if looking over the edge of an abyss.

Get back here! the Little Prince yelled. *Right now! Maddie, tell him to come—*

The journalist's head cocked towards the beach for a moment—had he heard? But he stayed where he was, and the dinghy had now floated past Maddie, out towards unencumbered ocean.

Fuck! Come on! The Little Prince took three steps towards the water, toes pushing against sand awkwardly. Then he looked behind him. His colleague was shaking his head.

I can't swim, he said.

The hell you can't!

You were the one watching him.

Maddie! the Little Prince shouted once, and then he was in the water, his pants flailing around his legs, struggling into a swimming position even as the ocean floor beneath him refused to dip. It was like moving through syrup. Maddie looked back at him, her face indecipherable. Amused? Confused?

Get him ba—! The rest of the Little Prince's words were lost in guzzled seawater. Hacking, he swam on. With the loss of daylight came the loss of any sense of distance. In the fog of his mind, the Little Prince realized that his cell phone was still in his pants. *Fuck.* He increased his exertions. He stayed focused on the tiny little scrap of the dinghy visible to him. An invisible line was connecting him to it, and pulling him towards it, so hard that it was tearing his consciousness away from his body. Now he was caught up in the back-pull of small waves which were pushing him out, just like the journalist was getting pushed out. He was just about up to Maddie now, except she was pulling ahead, because she had divined what was happening and was swimming towards the dinghy. He couldn't get his head up high enough to get a good view of what the journalist was doing. Was he passed out? Had he started paddling? What was he thinking?

Come on! Maddie called back to the Little Prince. *I think the boat's sinking!*

He heard something that sounded like a little pop, like a firework that detonates in demure fashion, except instead of sparks, he saw the journalist's arms splashing above the water, stretching up towards a blood-red moon that wasn't there. He was a rock 'n' roller offering a salute before diving off the stage and into the crowd. The Little Prince took a breath and hurled himself towards the journalist in a sloppy jackknife that crashed him into the incoming waves.

* * *

Hey you, the woman at the desk said. *Hey.*

The Little Prince had been dreaming. It was one of those dreams in which distance had no meaning, and you stepped out of a familiar place in your neighborhood to find yourself in another place thousands of miles away. He was hanging with his high school friends in the bones of what would become a multi-level parking lot, Dust, cool concrete ground, canvas, protection from curious eyes— just what they wanted. They were passing cigarettes around, not talking intelligently about anything at all. In fact, they were mostly laughing. It was a relief to be inconsequential, to not consider the very real problems of their lives. Then in the next moment he was in Berlin. It had been the only time he had been outside the country, his one free night away from Party Youth convention activities. He had found himself in a beer hall that burned with smoke and electric neon. The floor was sticky with spilled drinks, men and women had tattoos crawling up their necks, the music was concussive techno. He thought at the moment: *This is like a movie happening in real life, right in front of me.* He was looking out a window, but instead of a cityscape he saw a moonlit beach before him, and the blankness of the scene terrified him. He wanted to tear himself away from it, and yet he was already beyond the window, as if it had never existed, and rushing headlong into the sand, into nothingness.

Hey! the woman said, again.

He was fully awake. He was back in the capital, in the hospital. He looked for his cell phone to check the time, then remembered that he hadn't replaced it yet. The clock above the receptionist told him that he had been in the waiting room for an hour. Incredible. They needed an hour to verify him to see his own father. But that might have been the point—ever since his father had fallen out of favor, contact with others, even family members, had to be regulated. Or maybe that was paranoia speaking. Nobody had actually told him this was the case. But what else could it be? That was the trick, wasn't it? If you get to the point where you think there might a reason behind everything, then the reason exists, whether it actually does or not.

Come on, the receptionist said. *You were yelling at me an hour ago to see him, what are you dawdling for?*

He bit his tongue as he approached the desk. She thrust a new set of papers at him.

I already signed—

We just got these.

He stared at the papers. They seemed official enough—some sort of release form. Was he surrendering something by signing them? It didn't matter; he had surrendered everything else. He remembered what the journalist had told him: *I don't have belongings any more. All I have is what I write in the space of a day, and sometimes even that is lost. And that's fine, because you start every day clean.*

The Little Prince said: *I need to borrow a pen.*

The woman at the desk gave him a brief glare, as if to say, *You are more annoying then you'll ever know, but I will muster up a surpassing amount of patience to deal with you at this moment.* Then she tossed a ballpoint onto the desk in front of him. He started signing each page as directed, very methodically, and within a few seconds she was clicking her tongue. *Hurry up, hurry up,* she snapped. She held her hand out for her pen.

Hurry up, what's this hurry up shit? the Little Prince shouted. *I'm not some fucking dog!*

She made a sound that could have been surprise, shock, or maybe even a little amusement, and that only served to infuriate him more. He finished signing, shoved the papers at her, and then threw the pen at the desk. It bounced impressively into the air, then disappeared beyond. He half-expected her to order him to pick it up, but he had had enough and was already walking down the hall, down to the room where his father was, as he had many times in the recent past.

His father and the room had been exactly how he had left him a few weeks before, except for the bouquet of flowers by the window that had rotted entirely since the last time. His father's face and chin were above the sheet; under the sheet, his limbs were stalk-like, faint. They hadn't shaved his father's chin for a few days at least, and the gray gristle there made him look even older than he was.

Good morning, Dad, he said. His father's eyes were open, his chest was atremble with breath, but he didn't respond, same as every other time he had come to visit since the last stroke.

I never thought I looked like you, and I don't look like you now, thought the Little Prince. He sat down by his father's side and gave him a pat on the shoulder. It was like there was no shoulder there, just an arm that ended abruptly. The ventilation system in the room was rattling—there was a screw loose somewhere. The air had the smell of rubbing alcohol. *Better air than that beach hotel,* thought the Little Prince.

Dad, I have to take you home today. Just saying those words was difficult. It was as if he was invoking something. He envisioned his father lying in bed at home, staring at the ceiling, unresponsive, whilst relatives squabbled and debated in the next room, smoking their cigarettes. Ever so slowly, all the smoke and carcinogens would work their way under the bedroom door, through the walls, and swamp his father, accelerating his decline. It would be like that for a while, and then finally all bodily movement would cease and his father's stare would lock onto the ceiling for good, or at least until somebody came to remove the body. What was happening today was merely a step in the chain. All he was doing was moving the corpse to another place so it could become what it was always meant to be.

I'm sorry, he said. *I fucked up. I fucked it all up. Because of that, they won't take care of you anymore.* It would be much easier if his father could just look at him. Even if his father wasn't aware of him, just looking at him would be enough for him to dissimulate, and imagine that he was paying attention. Or if he knew his father would rouse himself from his coma, he could write this all down, leave it by his bedside, and when he awoke he would read about what had happened instead of having someone else explain it to him. He had to throw those flowers out. Even though they were leaving the room anyway, he couldn't bear the sight of them. A hospital should be honest, and keep its rooms completely bare. They belong to no one, for no one stays there for long.

The hospital back at the beach had it right: just white walls, blinds, bed frames of metal and canary bedsheets, and just outside the journalist's window, a friendly grouping of trees that made the sound of the surf when the wind blew through them. The Little Prince had told the staff, *The moment this man wakes up, let me know. And please do not engage in conversation, no photos, no phones.* The staff had nodded agreeably. Even they seemed to understand: *This place is merely a way station, so why get snippy or irritated about anything?* When the Little Prince was ushered in, the journalist had already been propped up in a seated position, looking hearty indeed after a fresh shave, his hair shampooed and combed back. The TV was on, and for a moment the Little Prince realized: *Shit, today is National Day*—but the journalist wasn't watching any parades or speeches. Instead he had tuned into a game show rerun, someone hitting someone else on the head with a rubber mallet. He was too busy wolfing down congee, eggs and smelly durian anyway. *No matter what happens to you, you must eat. That is an incontrovertible fact*, he told the Little Prince.

You're lucky I'm not going to report what you did, the Little Prince said.

Oh? Why not?

Because I would be in deep shit.

But the hospital has a record.

They have a record of your stay, but the Party doesn't need to know.

What about your buddy? Isn't he going to say something?

I talked to him. "Talk" was a strong word. Rather, they communicated without speaking too much. The Little Prince bought a pack of cigarettes and lit one up for the first time in years. His colleague smoked as well, the both of them standing outside the hospital, awaiting word on the journalist's condition, butts scattered at their feet.

We should have both been more attentive, the Little Prince said, finally.

You were watching him, his colleague said.

We were both watching him.

You decided to take him out.

And you came along.

Neither said anything for a period. Finally, the Little Prince's colleague scratched at the back of his ear, as if he was embarrassed. *I need money for getting back home*, he said.

But you were given a stipend to cover that. That was what the Little Prince was about to say, and then he understood. He almost asked him: *How much do you need?* But that was too bald-faced, much too unsubtle. So he dug out all the cash he had in his wallet, good enough for at least one vacation somewhere else, he reckoned, and offered it to him. *Here, this should cover it,* he said.

Oh, no, his colleague said. *I couldn't.* He pushed the Little Prince's money-stuffed hand away. This was the game: one makes an offer, the other couldn't possibly, but yes, the one making the offer is beneficence itself, like Buddha come down from Heaven, and the one accepting the offer must finally accept this token with the appropriate respect befitting such a gift. So his colleague took the money in the end, as stone-faced as ever, and the Little Prince hated the man because he hated himself for having to do this, but at least that part was over and the rest would be formalities.

I hate hospitals, the journalist said. *I don't know why. I don't spend much time in them, why should I have an opinion?*

If you hate them, said the Little Prince, *then you shouldn't have nearly gotten drowned.*

I say what I'm not supposed to say, why wouldn't I do what I'm not supposed to do?

Were you trying to escape?

Ha! I'm not that dramatic. I don't know. I guess I just wanted to see where the waves would take me.

You said you hated the water.

Yep. But you gotta try shit occasionally. You know what my favorite place is?

No. The Little Prince was past minding the journalist's meanderings at this point. The crisis had been averted, he would stay here in the hospital with him for the duration, and everything would be all right. The bastard could say anything he wanted to.

Out west, near the desert, you have these small towns, said the journalist. *Nothing to do but play dice all night. Do people from your generation still play dice? I'd hate to think that habit is going extinct. But it used to be so peaceful in those towns. Camels sleep in the streets. You think I'm smelly, you should get a load of the camels. But it's a warm kind of smelly. That's the word for everything out there. Warm. The people, the land. You help your neighbor out because you might need help from him tomorrow. That's just the way it is. Or the way it was, because it's all changing.*

Don't forget, I helped you out last night. It would have been a lot easier to let you drown.

That was more Maddie than you. Besides, you didn't want to let the Party down. You princelings have to look good against the Youth League newcomers. Factions against factions until the end of time. So how far along are you? Are you still a probational member? Part of a study group? Is this your final test?

It's a test, said the Little Prince.

Oh? How's that?

I'm here to prove my worth. My father is out of favor, but he's tried to keep me safe. Used what was left of his influence to get me this far. If I can prove I'm reliable, then I have a fresh start.

That's very unusual. Once the head of the family is out, the rest of the family…How did you manage it?

I proved I was ideologically pure.

The Little Prince stared at the TV. The game show was in full swing, one of the female contestants hiding her face in her hands after an egregious error, the host of the show mugging in disbelief at her *faux pas* before the camera, as if his life depended on it.

It's okay, the journalist said. *I know you can't tell me. You got secrets.*

I turned in the niece. The hotel manager's niece.

What?

It was anonymous, but I turned her in. She went crazy. We slept together once, and then she got it into her head that we'd be spending the rest of our lives together. Move to Hawaii or something. She thought my family was that powerful. So I tried to tell her we should just be friends, and she flipped. Started calling me around the clock. One minute she would be reasonable, the next minute she was screaming that I belonged to her.

Breakfast at Tiffany's, the journalist said.

Huh?

The big flaw with the end of the movie. When George Peppard says to Audrey Hepburn that she belongs to him. Just out of character, not romantic at all. Never mind, go on.

When I was accepted as a probationary member of the Party, I sent an email to all my friends letting them know the good news. She was on the email list, and she replied with just one sentence: GO TO HELL. She sent the reply to everyone. I was mad about that. Embarrassed. My father was falling out of favor at the time. I knew people were already doubtful about me. So I showed her email to the leaders of my local cell, and made the implication that her "Go to Hell" was referring to the Party.

You took care of two problems at once.

Yes.

Back in the Party's good graces, crazy girlfriend out of the picture.

She wasn't my girlfriend. I know they interrogated her. I don't know what happened after that. I just know she's alive, somewhere.

But she stopped communicating with you.

Yes. Probably ordered to cut off contact.

And here you are. Very ruthless.

I didn't think about it. I just did it.

Like I said.

A thermos of warm water had been laid out for the journalist, and the Little Prince grabbed it. He drank it all down.

The question is, said the journalist, *do you want to be in the Party?*

I told you, you have to be smart. The Party opens doors, and closes them.

Can I be honest? You haven't been very smart this weekend.

Yeah, no shit.

I mean, maybe it's because you're not into this.

Are you trying to draft me to your side?

I wouldn't presume. Just trying to get a read on you. It's important.

Nothing is important about me. If anything, you're important. And don't argue. That might be the only compliment I give you.

I won't. Don't worry. Your secret goes with me to my grave.

The Little Prince allowed himself a smile. *I thought you were the type that lives forever.*

No, I've got no illusions about that. But I know exactly how I want to go. After I'm dead, I want my body mummified inside a large pottery jar, in a sitting position. After a few months, you crack open the jar, you wash the body with alcohol, then you cover it in gauze, lacquer, and gold leaf. Then put me in a display case.

Are you serious?

They do it with monks. The belief is that your body only stays together through the mummification process if you're virtuous. If I could make it through that, it would be the highest honor for me. A good way to go.

You're crazy.

You have to make plans for the end in advance. You don't want to deal with it while you're going through it.

Why are you talking like you're dead? You have a fatal disease I don't know about?

Depends on your point of view. Maybe I should write up a final statement while I'm at it. You can be the witness. I'll wish the Great Leaders health for 10,000 years, and go back on everything I ever said. Then they'll definitely paint me in gold and throw me in a display case. What do you think?

I think, the Little Prince said, *we should have some whiskey.* He brought out the bottle with the unpronounceable Scottish name.

Save it for yourself. You'll need it more than me.

And that was it for meaningful conversation; the two of them sat in the room for the rest of the day watching game shows and action movie reruns. The actor who dubbed Arnold Schwarzenegger had gravel in his voice, like a wizened old master. The next morning, the Little Prince and his colleague escorted the journalist to the train station, where he was turned over to a fresh group of minders for the journalist's next destination, wherever that was. The new minders were the Little Prince's age, and a much more sober group. The journalist made as if to shake the Little Prince's hand, then thought the better of it given the present assembly, and instead tossed a jaunty salute. And that was the last the Little Prince saw of him.

But it wasn't the last of the story—as he sat by his father in the hospital room, he started laughing, for several reasons. For one, since he had no cell phone, his girlfriend in the capital couldn't get in touch with him, which was just fine with him. And because he had no cell phone, he didn't get the news until he returned to the capital, when he was informed that an anonymous Twitter account had been set up on National Day, with a single tweet: *How I spent my #NationalDay with an illustrious Party member.* The journalist had signed the post with another hashtag: his name. Accompanying the tweet was a photo of the journalist and the Little Prince, both of them on those beach chairs in front of the bar, the journalist with the grin of a wolf as he held up two beer bottles, one of them clanking against the Little Prince's drink, which sat in the Little Prince's near-comatose hand. The Little Prince's face was facing the camera phone, lids heavy, mouth dumbly open.

The bastard, thought the Little Prince when he saw the tweet for the first time. So simple: he chose the right moment, with the Little Prince all but passed out, and his colleague taking a piss. He had Maddie take the photo with her phone, then she posted the tweet later. Did she know him after all? Did he get in touch with her before he arrived, and they somehow engineered all of it? He would never know the answer—she disappeared shortly after he returned to the capital. The owner of the beach bar only knew her by her English name, and she had never shown him her resident identity card (she was only temporary help after all). Of course it could also have meant that she was used to drifting around, and as promised, she had moved on.

And so that was where matters now stood, both he and his father heading home in disgrace. His father's finish was preordained: it might take a few weeks, or a few months, but he would remain in their apartment until the end. Disciplinary action for the Little Prince would require some time to formulate. In the meantime, no Party activities, no contact with people outside the Party. On the other hand, stepping out into the street would now bring a pang of thrilling anxiety: Was someone watching him? Making sure he wasn't in communication with dissidents or irritants? He was suddenly important, like the journalist. The journalist would never be seen again. A few fellow activists would point out this fact, and a woman would step forward to demand his whereabouts—whether she was his wife or his mistress, the Little Prince never paid enough attention to confirm. Soon there would be more prominent dissidents to campaign about, and changes in leadership and national economic plans to discuss.

After his father's death, the Little Prince would walk aimlessly around the capital, the smog rendering the streets as impressionist paintings. Sometimes a passerby would look at him for a second longer than necessary, and the Little Prince would wonder: *Does he recognize me from the Twitter photo?* Of course the Twitter account had been deleted, but not until the day after the original post. Surely a sizable number of people had saved the photo, passed it on along their own networks. Electrons firing fast as light, unstoppable. He would settle for something a little slower, like a motorcycle, a BMW knockoff like the one the journalist had. The thought would remind him of something the journalist said during their last night in the hospital, as they watched Arnold Schwarzenegger on TV, the muscleman darting on his motorcycle along Los Angeles streets, a sawed-off shotgun like a toy in his hands. *The only thing you need in this world is a motorcycle,* the journalist murmured. *You can load a motorcycle with anything. Clothes, cookies, milk powder, even televisions. You can ride hundreds of kilometers on those suckers without so much as a hiccup. That's all you need out in the hinterlands. Distances are vast and the roads are horrible, but the motorcycle can handle it. Break free from your terrible job, head for the mountains, head anywhere else. All is possible with a motorcycle. It should be a law: Need to get away from it all? You must get yourself a motorcycle.* And standing in the streets of the capital months later, the Little Prince would remember those words, and come to realize that the journalist knew that all this would happen, and was offering him one last piece of advice.

But smoggy streets and travel and motorcycles would all be in the future. For now, he laughed at his father's bedside, in front of a man who betrayed not a trace of cognizance, who was never given to laughing. *We were both stupid,* said the Little Prince. *That's all I needed to say, but now you can't hear me say it.* With a tenderness that was a surprise to him, he bent down to stroke the older man's head. It was probably the first time he had touched him in years. *That bar on the beach is still there,* he said.

He had gone to the bar straight from the train station after dropping off the journalist, to find Maddie there. A tuxedo cat had wandered over, and it was snug and purring in her lap. Was it the old cat from his younger days? Impossible, but he called it Panda anyway. Captain and Tennille were back on the jukebox, preserved in their recurrent loop. He and Maddie cracked open the bottle of whiskey the journalist had been so keen on buying, and sat in the tattered beach chairs a final time. It wasn't the greatest whiskey, in the Little Prince's view—a bit too much peat taste for his liking.

Is he all right? Maddie asked of the journalist, and the Little Prince said he was fine, just fine. *Good,* she said, serene as always, and let out a sigh that seemed to draw all the air around them into it. She really was beautiful, but somehow he knew even at that moment that this was as far as the relationship would go. Not that he dared to think she would be an easy mark for him—he was just feeling magnanimous. *You will be spared from all my shit.* So all he said was: *I still can't believe we're getting this weather at this time of year.* The tallow trees rocked with the wind, casting shadows on the ground that swayed and grasped, and they sat there with shots in hand, looking out at the sea and the faint formations of what might have been incoming clouds.

TABLEAU

SATURDAY MORNING AT 11:03 BEGINS, AS IT always does, with Nat King Cole and "Walkin' My Baby Back Home." Outside the café, a van bounces by with a hiccup of white smoke. The scattering, adorable little footsteps of children are heard but not seen. So it was, so it is now, so it will be.

The café does not exist anymore, nor does the van, the children, the turntable in the corner upon which the Nat King Cole record spins round and round. Yet here they are, every component of 11:03 a.m. present and accounted for. She sits alone in the center of the café, facing slightly away from the door so as to grant herself a bit of privacy. It is the optimal location between the café's stereo speakers. Nat croons about a late night with his baby. The waiter places coffee cup, spoon and saucer just a few centimeters beyond her right hand resting on the table. She doesn't look at him; she has never looked at him, so she can't start now. If she did look at him she would notice that it is not always the same waiter who serves her, but the cup and saucer are always placed in the same position.

It wasn't too long ago (she flatters herself it wasn't too long ago, even though it was at least decades previous) that she was in a foreign land and found herself in this café, or rather, a café exactly the same as this. An unremarkable café overall, but something about the white lace curtains, the daintiness of the porcelain, the way the sun played across the walls and the breeze stole in to ruffle the napkins, reminded her of even earlier days, when her world was cobbled streets and fields under crisp autumn skies, long before palace intrigue and chauffeured rides and glimpses of faces in multitudes of crowds. Happy with her anonymity here, she drinks her mocha in two sips. It tastes the same, then and now.

Here the record skips for a second and a half, just before the line about walking arm in arm, as it always must. Back when there were millions of LPs, the man who was once a journalist collected them. Albums at his home were catalogued by genre and artist, entire walls devoted to his pursuit. He had a talent (he would say curse) for cataloging and recalling everything: conversations, sights, even the smells of a place.

One day in a foreign land, preoccupied with the notion that he would never write something original, that he would forever be a chronicler and not an artist, the journalist found himself in a café. He sank into a seat in the corner, swarmed by his thoughts, all track of time lost. The next thing he knew, it was an hour later and he was the only customer left. The turntable was repeating the first track from Nat King Cole's "The Billy May Sessions." Then, just before the line about walking arm in arm, the record skipped for about one and a half seconds, the equivalent of a breath. It was enough to snap him back to the world.

And that was that, the incident dormant in his mind, until years later. After all the wars, long after that foreign land had been razed, its population dispersed, long after

TABLEAU 143

there was a need for journalists, some very polite men had sought him out. Yes, he had been in that particular café on that date. Yes, he could recall the details of the café. After all, his mind was nothing more than a bloody recording device. No, better than that, he was assured—not only could he observe, he could also *discern*, and discernment was paramount.

It is 11:04, and the moment in Nat's musical tale in which the woman snuggles her head on his chest. The fly enters, as it always does. A fat bauble razzing and buzzing, it skirts past her ear and settles on her bare left arm. Human and fly gaze at each other for a few moments, sizing each other up. Then with a swish of her napkin, her arm is covered, the offending beast trapped. A brief application of pressure, and the fly is crushed. Dots of blue and red soak the napkin where it was. She stares at the spot, as if she is the one exterminated, and is more keenly aware of life than she has ever been.

Since flies no longer thrive in this part of the world, fresh batches must be constantly flown in. They are trained for months, and even with all the thousands to work from, only one or two at a time gain enough skill to qualify for the honor of undertaking that predetermined suicide mission from doorway to arm. The mocha is equally rare (black market, fees still within reason), as is the turntable (under the perfect replica housing, a Frankenstein of circuits from a half-dozen dead components), as is the van that passes by (since she never actually sees the van hurtle past, one need only replicate the noise of the motor, the specific ingredients of its exhaust smoke, the impression of a vehicle moving from left to right), as is the Nat King Cole album (a mint version unearthed from the journalist's collection, with a scratch of specific length and depth applied at a precise position, so as to create that second-and-a-half skip).

It is the former journalist's job to ensure that everything in this café happens as it must. The weight of the lace curtains as well as their look must be judged, so they always billow the same when the artificially-generated breeze blows through. The cuffs on the waiter's sleeves must eternally be buckled just so. Even the aggregated smell of the morning's fresh baked goods must be fabricated—it is a tricky thing, manufacturing a scent that is indeterminate yet spot-on. Every week is devoted to rehearsal, preparation, evaluation, all for that moment at 11:03 a.m. every Saturday when she is seated, the song plays, the mocha is delivered, the song skips, the fly arrives, the fly is extinguished.

At the next table over, a college boy and girl murmur to each other. For a few moments she listens. *It's just better not to talk*, the girl says. *Half the time you're not thinking when you talk, and the other half gets misinterpreted anyway.* He teases her back: *What if you're a good listener? You gonna discriminate against good listeners with your silence?* These words are spoken in a foreign language which she will never understand—not that she cares. (Just like the cover of a book, the journalist muses—sometimes you fall in love with a cover, and engaging with the actual contents would be a letdown.) Reconstituting this conversation required interviews with survivors and relatives as well as tireless linguistic research, and then it was a matter of finding correct actors for the roles, at least until they outgrow them, whereupon new actors will be recruited, and repeat, and again. For now, it is enough for the boy and girl to play their drama for the woman's benefit. She detects love behind their words (or at least imagines so, it is open to debate as to whether they actually loved each other), and smiles. On cue, another breeze scuttles across the room.

TABLEAU 145

She absently clears her hair around her forehead, caught up in the simple pleasure of it all—mocha, tissue on arm, boy and girl laughing at each other, breeze, and Nat's next verse: the woman is afraid of the dark, so he must park outside her door till the morning light.

She is unaware of the journalist's existence. They must never meet, because that would introduce subjectivity, and interfere with the integrity of what has been created and reinforced. She is attractive, she is known to many—apart from this, all he knows of her is contained within the café. Two sips of mocha. Fly on arm. Smile at boy and girl. Hundreds of times he has witnessed this scene, and yet, somehow, all that occurs happens as it always has. It is akin to watching a trapeze artist. He is mesmerized by the spectacle, by her.

She wants nothing more from life than to replicate this one moment of happiness, drown in it. Why not drugs? Virtual reality? No, he has been told, nothing matches the tactile. Movements through time leave more of an imprint on memory. She is past caring about public opinion or legacy. Her recollections have been transferred to him through third parties and married with his own remembrances, the accumulated knowledge codified in notebooks, outlines, draftsman's contracts. He is often reminded of something a fellow journalist said once: *History is written by those who take the time to write it.* He is regressing from journalist to historian. At this rate, nothing he does will ever be his own. And yet, it is clear this is his talent.

She is given a snack: peanut butter brittle with wasabi sprinkles. She cracks a piece in half and swallows, whereupon her hand goes to her throat. Something caught there, just for a moment. A whole peanut seed. It is of no concern, at least none related to health. She swallows hard again, seed released, and she imagines it will tumble into her stomach, where it will take root and grow. How wonderful it would be. *Silly*, she says out loud. As always, no one notices her outburst. Everyone in the café is aware of it, of course, but no one can betray that they have noticed.

At 11:06 a man enters the café. It is not known then or now who the man was. He sits in the corner, near the turntable, forming a vertex equidistant from doorway and cashier. The woman's back is completely to him. She remembers this event because she can smell his cologne. Woods and waterfalls. Her spoon is in her hand, poised to stir her fresh cup of mocha, and she considers turning , even for just an instant, to look at him. It seems preordained. Nat King Cole, mocha, fly, boy and girl, fresh breeze, peanut seed. This should be the next event in this crucial chain. But she is exhausted; much to do, many responsibilities to honor, and she is not used to entertaining so many idle thoughts. Not even the mocha and the dead fly on her arm can forestall sleep. She has heard of a spoon siesta, where one takes a nap with spoon in hand, and when the spoon drops from your grasp to the floor it is time to wake up. Content with that knowledge, she sits, and waits, her eyes closed.

The journalist sits in the corner. It is not his first time there, and others have taken his position in the past, but he is there now, fulfilling the historical imperative of What Really Happened. He knows one thing more, though. He was in that corner so long ago, in that café in a foreign land, behind her. He wasn't aware of this, of her, back then—it was the one time he had refused to pay attention to the world, to catalogue. But he has come to realize that it was him. He cannot divulge this fact; if he did it would break this loop, change her irrevocably. The café would no

TABLEAU 147

longer exist, and he would no longer have an opportunity to play this part, to sit in the corner, to watch her, watch the spoon poised between her fingers, watch her lips go soft as she becomes drowsy and invites dreams that will not come true.

For the last time in the song, Nat sings about walking his baby back home.

The spoon drops.

Trio

CHARACTERS:

Two men, one woman, all in late twenties or early thirties—their features will remain the same while the accoutrements (hair, clothes) change, contingent on the character that they are playing. In relation to the setting (see below), they are the kind of folk who may be from the same country, but are not local.

Setting:

A sleepy town near the ocean, in the Asian tropics. Key feature: it feels out of time, or rather, unbothered by the concept of time. A vacation getaway that has seen better days, or has yet to see them. Buildings and bungalows that are in disrepair, but can seem romantic if you squint hard enough. Streets ramshackle with rental bicycles gathering dust, signs bleached blue from the sun. A local single-screen theater built into the auditorium of an abandoned youth center, the air conditioning rattling like insane bees.

A few locals who play into the narrative in various ways:

The pouty teenage girl at the convenience store who isn't really as sullen as she appears, just bored bored bored, far too narcotized by the nothing around her to be aware that her demeanor shields her from anything interesting.

The elderly woman who runs the noodle shop (any place worth documenting has a noodle shop, a *good* noodle shop, natch), a bit gruff and smothering in her attitude, but it all comes from a place of love, much like the steam of noodle soup can be off-putting when it's fresh from the kitchen and hits you in the eye, before you come to recognize, accept, and savor.

At night:

The town balances on the precarious edge between sleep and dream. A few smatterings of neon lights which can be interpreted as scuzzy in certain contexts, romantic in others. A single all-purpose bar/club/dance hall that may have karaoke one night, disco and glitterballs the next. The sound of the sea is a demure yet constant presence. Sodium streetlamps give off a gutsy, grainy glow, and hint at mysteries better left alone.

The beach:

Not the happy crystalline sort found in travel magazines, but it does have a certain charm once you settle in under the wilting palms and it is explained to you that the churn of the water, all chocolate-brown, is merely due to a recent thunderstorm (once all settles down, the ocean will return to a shade short of azure, yet perfectly respectably blue in its own way, like the blue in someone's eyes after a long life, well-lived). At one far end of the beach litter is piled high, most of it carried in by the currents, dragged down to this point from all sides of the coast.

The highlands:

Moving away from town and sea, the roads are lush with tall green grasses and bamboo. During the day, in the moments when the sun is hidden behind clouds, the hills have the unreality of a children's book. In the evening, when the sun dips low and getting lost on the footpaths that lead through these jungles and groves becomes a very real danger, one can picture a pursuit, an escape, the possibility that all may be lost. Then there are the temples or abandoned spiritual retreats, choked with dead leaves, the tendrils of weeds, the stone steps cracked and all the more enticing because of it, the interiors always bristling with incense no matter the time of day or year, gilded statues of Buddhas trapped in glass cases. And a little bit beyond these temples is a modest little tiled building that houses guest rooms and hot spring baths inside, the smell of sulfur burned into the walls. The proprietor constantly sniffs his nose, and runs the place with spectacular disinterest, so much so that one might wonder if he does so to protect the secrets and whims of whoever comes to visit: Adulterous affairs? Criminal activities? Someone who needs to get away from something for a while?

Structure:

Omnibus film, containing three stories. Each story will have its own tone, its own rhythm, its own ground to tread. The common thread is the location and the actors playing the main characters, even though the characters change from story to story.

Music:

Story 1 will have a soundtrack propulsive with jazz and blues, underscoring the action, or pushing it to the brink of parody, given the characters' potential delusions in this segment. At the finish, a long-underrated pop song will appear, with an ironic twist: a character comments early on how he hates that song, yet finds himself pulled into the emotions of the moment when the song finally plays, first on a tinny high-band boom box on a café table, then expanding into full fidelity.

Story 2 will make use of diegetic sound. The faraway cries of seagulls. The spluttering trucks that lumber down the town's main street, ten years too old and carrying a few hundred pounds too much weight. The peculiar invigorating crack of sandals on a gravel road. The stereophonic whoosh of the wind at night, as it moves from right to left, from sea to shore. The story concludes with a musical piece that rises above the ambience, something minimal like Avro Pärt or Harold Budd. Perhaps the defining song of Story 1 returns, but in a different variation. Think of the theme in Altman's *The Long Goodbye*.

Story 3 will fall between the approaches of Story 1 and 2: mostly ambient and environmental sound for the most part, with music during the flashback sequences and the conclusion. Story 3 could be a musical, to match the more operatic scope. One can see a finale in which all the townspeople join our main characters in a swooping number that carries them through the streets and out to the seashore for the finale.

Cinematography:

Story 1: Fast-paced, shots and sequences timed with the action or comedy on screen. Aggressive cuts and pans. Close-ups and dutch angles allowed.

Story 2: Naturalistic in lighting, with framing mostly medium shots. Long tracking shots following the characters as they move in and out of each others' orbits.

Story 3: Saturated with color and shadows, the story takes place within the span of a single evening. Faces prevail over surroundings, to the point that every blurred movement in the background could be a whispering curtain, a figure that may or may not exist.

Synopses:

Story 1: Tropic Noir
Who is who?

Sweltering summer weather, noir-like with sweat. A man (lead male actor #2) has arrived in town, alone, minus baggage, his eyes hawk-like and on the lookout for trouble. He is dressed simply and formally—black shirt, slacks, leather shoes, and a fedora hat. In short, entirely out of place in this sleepy town. He is meticulous in everything: the snap of his wrist to consult the time, the notes he writes to himself in tidy shorthand, the way he hangs his clothes in the hotel closet, each item equidistant from the next. Within moments he stows his gear, changes into a relaxed tropical shirt, and hits the town. At first glance, he might appear to be a hard-boiled man with a soft-boiled conscience, or a hired gun (itinerary of an assassin, perhaps?).

We see the streets through his eyes, pregnant with surprise, excitement, mystery. A stray cat padding its way down the sidewalk could be a harbinger of death. The man lounging on a stool, staring in our protagonist's direction, could be a wrong one. [To us, it's clear he's just a drunk.] The locals regard the stranger with curiosity, in the way that locals will eye any visitor who is calibrated differently than everyone else. His first stop is the convenience store, where he tries chatting up the girl at the counter. He is not without charm, even if it's of the overdetermined Don Juan sort, but the girl continues to pop her bubble gum and stare at her magazine on the counter.

That chewing gum you like will come back in style, he jokes.

What? she says.

That's a line from a TV show.

Oh. Unimpressed.

The man receives a phone call, sparing him further humiliation. It's a one-sided conversation, with someone from a far-off city, we gather, someone who's not shy about browbeating him. *Still haven't found him yet? I wish you were at least a piece of shit, because then maybe he'd slip on you and you'd find him that way!* The boss-man on the other end of the line is insistent: this missing man, this scum who deserves everything that's coming to him, must be found. The man allays the boss's concerns with soothing words. He is no tough guy, but neither does he seem incompetent. Everything in its time. During his travels he has assembled the information he needs. The missing man is said to be laying low in this town with his girlfriend, as far from things as you can get on this continent. It is said that they hang out at the local noodle shop. Everyone ends up at the noodle shop. The convenience store girl provides him directions to the restaurant with a few vague motions of her index finger.

Late afternoon: The man has stationed himself inside the noodle shop. Beer cans and spent cigarettes pile up on his table as he waits. The hunched old woman who runs the shop eyes him with suspicion; any man who drinks instead of eating noodles here cannot be trusted. He accepts her hostility as part of his job—for every unfamiliar place, there will be an unfriendly stare. A woman (the film's female lead) enters. She is dressed in the latest fashions of the city, adapted for a weekend beach getaway: a gossamer top, black slacks hugging her bottom, just the right amount of mascara and blush to enforce the illusion of a natural look. It is clear she is also a stranger in town. Two strangers in her noodle shop—the old woman can no longer keep silent, so she hectors the man. *Where you from? What you doing here? You wanna talk to her?* Alarmed that his anonymity may be blown, he beats a quick retreat back down the road, where he waits. As if on cue, the town's streetlamps bloom to life, and those old dusty shopfronts grow languorous with shadows.

Finally the woman leaves the noodle shop, and he trails her down the quiet streets. He is entranced by the way she walks; how she throws her hair out carelessly. Eventually she leads him to the local cinema, oldies night, and they are the only two people at the theater. Once again he is staring at the back of her head, and the sight is somehow haunting, even as the movie (a crime melodrama) blares at them.

After the movie, he trails her to the local club, which is rigged with video monitors for karaoke night. Random locals are hogging the mike, but soon they relinquish the stage to the woman, who vamps on an old tune, something from decades before, a sultry love song. She doesn't oversell it; instead she twists ever so slightly with the lyrics, as if channeling a long-dead star. Watching from a safe distance, the man is transfixed. *Veronica Lake. That's who she reminds me of.*

Just as he is thinking this, pleased with the notion, she walks straight over to his table, gaze unwavering, pulls out a chair, and deposits herself on it. *You look like a tourist,* she says.

So do you, he grins.

Are you just as bored with this town as I am?

Yes. But with my brains and your looks, we could go places.

Is that from a movie?

The Postman Always Rings Twice. *Sorry. I learned all my moves from old movies.*

Which starts a conversation about favorite old films, and some shared ground, although they disagree about *Laura*: he loves it, she finds it creepy. He buys piña coladas, and she lights her cigarette in a bored manner. At one point one of the karaoke singers tackles a more recent, plush little pop song, with lyrics concerning lost, avoided love. He winces, she notices. *What's wrong with a sweet pop song now and again?* she says.

Too sappy. Give me an old standard any day, he replies.

Soon they're out of old song and old movie talk, and she points out that he has asked her nothing about who she is and why she is a visitor here.

A trumpet burns on the club speakers. *I like coming up with stories about people before I get to know them,* he says.

Sounds like you create a lot of disappointment for yourself.

But someday my imagination will match reality, and when that happens... He toasts the air.

So what am I?

Spontaneously, he comes up with this scenario: How about a comedy? She is a flighty heiress, toing-and-froing about the country, but urgent business back in the city requires her immediate attention, otherwise her financial security is at risk. And he is a troubleshooter hired by a competitive firm, who needs to track her down and engineer matters so her own relatives won't find her in time. And of course, in the process of hanging around with her and getting to know her... He doesn't articulate the last part, but that's the way these stories go.

So you've been hired to keep an eye on me, she says.

Yes. In this scenario.

And if I run?

Grinning at the implied challenge, he answers: *I have to keep up. I guess.*

Fine—then come on!

And before he can respond, she is out of her chair, so fast that even as he turns his head to follow, he can only see her hair as it bounces in good-bye, as if she has expertly maneuvered herself out of the camera frame. She is out of the club, and walking down the street. With a few stumbles, he pursues, catches up. What's her game here? Surely she must at least suspect that he is after her boyfriend. This could all be a ruse, designed to ensnare him. Excellent. What is a noir without these story turns?

They make a stop at the local convenience store (the girl at the counter who so grudgingly obliged with information earlier in the day is still there, and impressed by the sight of the two of them—*Maybe this guy isn't all empty talk,* she thinks). The woman purchases a bottle of vodka and a frying pan. *You need a frying pan where you're going?* he asks.

You said I'm a little crazy.

And so they wander around town, surrendering to the rhythm of a warm summer night. Outside the club, close to her now, close to her bare neck, he smells her perfume. It's like a powerful anesthetic. She quizzes him on his past, what he's done, who he's been with. He refuses to surface many details, yet the little bits of information he relays suggest a life lived at the behest of others, when not being thrown this way and that by debts and bad relationships. He shrugs it all off in the tough-guy way he imagines

Bogart would.

Maybe you should do something for yourself, she muses.

Nope, I've got too many obligations to strike out on my own, he says.

It's simple to start something. Watch. And with impeccable timing she jumps aboard a passing bus (which only happens by once an hour) for the mountains, he diving in just behind, but not without an unfortunate encounter with a closing door and his leg. The bus bops up and down, side-to-side, as it winds its way upward, and there is something serene about her as she looks out the window at the growing darkness, quiet and content, even as the bounces make him carsick. Just to pass the time, he asks her where she's going next. She tells of distant countries, friends and opportunities, a chance to think differently, live differently. (Is she getting into character, or finally revealing herself? He can't say.) She imagines herself on a city street far away, someplace foreign and vibrant, amongst the human swarm and energized by it, and we see her vision: standing amidst the crowds in a neon wonderland, the slightest of satisfied smiles on her face as life whips by her at double-speed.

It is a dodge-and-parry, their dialogue, matching the erratic, uneven motions of the bus. *So what happens when this is over?* she asks. *You just go back? Continue being someone else's lapdog?*

You have another option?

We could go somewhere else. The bus rocks, her head bobs up and down in invitation.

I'm just supposed to keep watch over you. That's all.

That's very professional. I like it when people play it cool. Just makes it all the better when you get hot.

He laughs at that one. *If you say so,* he says.

Eventually the bus comes to its last stop: a near-empty hot spring hotel squatting just within a bamboo forest. *Want to come up for a bit?* she says.

And now we come to it, he thinks. Is her boyfriend here? Is he laying in ambush? Or is he somewhere else entirely and this is just more misdirection? He could ask her about him, in a very off-handed way, but there would be nothing off-handed about it. It is his fault that he chose this particular scenario. Of course he could always adapt it—perhaps she is on the run with a man who she thinks loves her, but is merely interested in her money. A romantic rival. That would work.

His solution: delaying action. *I'll get some more drinks from the bar first.* So he seeks out the proprietor of the hotel—they're both from the same city, as it turns out—and they settle into easy conversation. *It's way more boring here,* the proprietor says, *but I don't care. We all find our place, and this is mine. The most excitement we get is when we make videos.* He shows off a set of monitors which have video feeds from hidden cameras in all the rooms. *Hot stuff on the Internet, you understand. Get a little extra money.*

The man bursts through the door of the woman's room to warn her, just as she is getting undressed. Taken by surprise, she responds by slugging him with the frying pan.

When he awakens she is watching over him, arms crossed, pan in hand, waiting for the explanation. He tells her about the cameras. *Thank you,* she says, massaging the bump on his head. *Such a spongy head,* she notes, then offers vodka. If her boyfriend was ever present, there is no sign of him now. Both clothed, both lounging on the bed, he still woozy, she feeling responsible and protective, they drain the bottle and observe the moon nosing upwards, just over the bamboo trees, the room a patchwork of light and shadows.

It is a lazy night and they feel it go by, rolling with it.

So we should talk about tomorrow, she says. *Don't get me wrong, tonight was fun, but I'm supposed to meet my brother tomorrow.*

He grunts in acknowledgment. So boyfriend is posing as brother. *I can come with you,* he says. *We can all hang out.*

I'm sure he'd like that. He still gets protective from time to time.

I'm sure he does, he thinks. What if they just went on the lam, just like those doomed couples in classic films? But it's never as romantic as it seems. It can't be. Maybe they could just be comrades on the run. But even comrades turn on each other in the movies.

So they make an arrangement: Tomorrow on the beach for brunch. Soon she is asleep, on her side and turned away from him, and he stares at the back of her once again, the strands of her Veronica Lake hair. He locks himself in the bathroom and phones the boss man. Tomorrow. Noon. All will be fixed. It is like admitting defeat, letting reality back into his life like this. He would much rather run off with this flighty heiress, and jet off to a happy ending. Does she feel the same? He could string the game out a little longer, and see between the two of them, who would break first and admit the truth of their position. He finishes what's left of the vodka, staring at the reflection of her sleeping face in the hotel window, and his face just above hers, just as stony. The air is fragrant with the sulfur from the hot spring baths that they never had a chance to try.

Next day: Brilliant sunshine, waves of stony blue lapping the sand. The man and woman are sitting on the beach, awaiting the "brother." The frying pan is at the woman's side. The beach is near-empty, save for a group of foreign tourists down at the water, raising a ruckus with their loud music and splashing. The juxtaposition of the two scenes—couple waiting quietly, tourists down at beach—intensifies in rhythm as the scene rolls.

Should be here soon, she says.

Yeah, he replies. One hand is deep in his pocket. There may or may not be something there, and she may or may not be noticing it. Both of them are playing this game to the end

Sure you don't want to make a getaway? she says.

We don't really know each other though, he replies.

Does it matter? What if it's just a fling? A fling can be good.

He's coming.

The "brother" (lead actor #1) is approaching from the beach parking lot. Fifty meters away, forty, getting closer. The man rises, hand still in pocket. He has positioned himself so he can see both the brother and woman, like the two other points on a triangle, and now the brother is drawing closer, closing up the triangle so that it is perfectly equilateral.

She throws him a smile. *It's funny*, she says. *Just about all the people I know were strangers when I met them.*

Now that *is Veronica Lake*, he laughs.

The brother has arrived. Like the woman, like the man, he is in tourist mode: suede slip-on shoes and white slacks. Both of his hands are in his pockets. For a long moment, the man and the brother look at each other. More screams from the tourists. A fresh wave crashes on the beachgoers, taking a few of them down.

Both the man and the brother say simultaneously to each other: *You're not him.*

What? she says.

This isn't my friend, the brother says.

This isn't the guy, the man says.

Both men take a step back, in perfect synch.

He was at the karaoke club, like you said he would be, the woman says to the brother.

You were at the noodle shop, the man says to her, *like they said you would be.*

Who are you? the brother says.

Are you really her brother?

Another step in retreat from both men. It is like they are preparing themselves for a proper duel, ten paces back.

Yes, I'm her brother.

He's not your boyfriend? he says to her.

What the hell— she begins.

I have a picture. Almost apologetically, the man swipes his phone unlocked, takes a few embarrassing seconds to find the correct photo, and shows it to the two of them. *I'm looking for this man.*

Both woman and brother shake their heads in unison.

Don't know him, the brother says. *And who are you? She was supposed to meet someone else last night.*

All together, all three of them say, *Are you...*

They stand in stunned silence.

A mistake has been made, the man says finally.

Yes, she agrees.

The brother says: *I'd like an explanation.*

I think it's best that we don't spend time on that, she says.

I agree, the man says.

The man and the woman look at each other. Both professional, both cool, both a little bit sad.

I guess you have something you need to do, she says.

And you, he says.

It was a nice evening.

It was something else.

All parties maintaining eye contact, they separate, the woman and her brother backing towards the parking lot, the man standing still, back to the sea. When they are a good twenty meters away, the man shouts out:

Maybe I'll live so long that I'll forget you. Maybe I'll die trying.

Puzzled, her mouth slightly open, she thinks for a moment. She says: *Out of the Past?*

He replies: *Lady from Shanghai.*

And with that she and her brother turn away. A new song is on the tourists' radio—the pop song that had annoyed the man the night before in the club. Slowly, a grin spreads across his face, an acknowledgment of his own foolishness, and then the smile flattens into something sad and knowing. He turns and walks down the beach, seemingly to nowhere, or maybe to the wall of trash piled up at the far end of the shore, as far from the tourists as possible. Then he stops, his gun in his hand, looking out to sea again, hypnotized by it. He closes his eyes. When he opens them again he is on a busy street in a country far away from everything he once knew, just like the woman was in her vision.

Story 2: Stopover

Running forward, or away?

Spring, verging on summer. A woman (female lead) has arrived in town, alone, burdened with a beat-up backpack and a digital SLR camera that can take photos and videos. From the outset it is apparent she is running away from something, or at least avoiding it. Her cell phone is always buzzing, with an insistently annoying pop song as its ring tone, but she never answers it or turns it off. Every time it rings she regards it as something she has stumbled upon, as if she is an amnesiac, striving to remember if she has left something important behind in memory and past life.

She wanders about the town, taking snapshots of everything – the bisecting lines of tiled roofs and sky, the shaggy street food, the scooters that zip to and fro. She tries filming some of the goings-on around town, but in a humorous sequence, she stations herself at various points, hoping for motion, happenings, *anything*, only to film a near-motionless street, an outdoor café devoid of people, a single truck taking forever to sputter from one side of the town's central square to the next. We don't see her in a hotel, or talking to the locals; she sits, she lounges on the beach, she loafs, the click of the camera and the ring of her cell phone the only constants. In one sequence we see her at the convenience store, picking up toiletries, studiously avoiding conversation with the pouty girl behind the counter, divorced from everything short of her bemused existence. In another she visits the local tea/travel shop, appraising the posters and brochures of other vacation spots, the plump man who owns and manages the place attentive, waiting, wanting to speak up at a few points, ask the relevant question: *Can I help you?* But he never does, and she never speaks. Often she looks up at a sky that is unchanging blue, in stasis.

After some time passes—a few days we reckon— another visitor arrives (lead male actor #1). He is also a traveler, burdened with a heavy backpack. He notices the woman, and she notices him, over breakfast, and they acknowledge each other, but little else. A little later, by chance, they're both in the city square around lunchtime, eating food from the same food stand: he has chicken, she has rice and vegetables. He sees her taking photos of her food and his mouth curls skeptically at the sight. Not too long after, the woman stumbles across the man, who is violently ill in an alley. He tries waving her off: *Something bad I ate*, he says. The woman insists on helping, and they both go to the local clinic, where the doctor, engrossed by the English premier football match on television (*Arsenal till I die, I'm Arsenal till I die!*), is slightly off the mark when he jabs him with antibiotics, the needle hitting a nerve, the man yelping.

The next few days the man is confined to bed in his hotel, and the woman stays with him, camped out on the floor, giving him water, making sure he's bundled up, while he's shivering with fever. They don't say much besides introducing themselves, the man thanking her, the woman demurring. *Where are you from?* he asks. *It doesn't matter*, she says. Still her cell phone rings, still she doesn't answer it.

Finally the man is healthy enough to be up and around, limping around (his leg is still sore from where it was jabbed with the needle), and the woman accompanies him around town. He wants to tell her where he's from, what he does, where he's going, but she refuses to let him do it. *If you have to talk about yourself, make something up*, she says. *Just pretend.*

And so they start making up stories about themselves, depending on the situation. To the tea/travel agency man they present themselves as eloping lovers, undecided on where to go to settle down, putting sly, undue pressure on the agent to come up with the ideal getaway. To the convenience store girl, they pose as inheritors of a small fortune, and proceed to buy every bit of liquid detergent, leading to a raucous afternoon on the sidewalks as they blow bubbles, the sidewalks becoming slick with soap, townspeople joining in, laughing all the way. To the old woman who runs the noodle shop (and thank goodness they don't have to make do with street food any more, it's noodles every day from here on out, now that they've discovered this place), they're long-lost relatives of someone in town. *Oh, tell me who he is! I'm sure I know him!* says the old woman. Caught up in the lie, they have to improvise, come up with certain memories, a certain age range, maybe one or two mutual friends, and by some miracle, the old woman lets out an *aha!* And steers them towards a lonely little house near the seashore, where a local man lives alone (male actor #2). The local man has recently lost his parents and is spending a lone summer in the house where he grew up, and even though he has no recollection of these two newcomers, he is in the mood to share drink, talk, even one of the spare bedrooms. He asks them about where they're from, and the man and woman continue to fabricate, spin tales of far-off cities, of life on the go, of trains and laptops and coffee.

And so the summer passes, the three of them at the beach, at the noodle house, at the local bar/karaoke club/ dance hall, not so much living out of time as much as ignoring it. They are now part of the town, part of the landscape, no longer simply observing. Their bodies grow limber and tan, seemingly intertwined everywhere they go, their smiles easy and unforced, their movements loose.

And inevitably, the story changes; the roles they have assumed begin to fall away. They are left with an irreducible situation: two men in love with one woman. They are all slow to recognize that this is happening, but moments that seem free and easy—who can get a drink first for the woman?—shade towards competition. Soon personal histories begin to leak out in individual discussions between each man and the woman, as if the men are saying to her, *This is the real me and you must get familiar with it because if we're to be together, we must have truth.* The woman chooses to ignore these signs at first (yes, she hates this passive-aggressive mode, but she is hoping against the odds that these moments will pass), and as a defense, she continues to take photos at every opportunity, judging it far better to document than to engage. The images from her camera are as sun-drenched as ever, but their faces in these images grow pinched. As the days stretch towards summer and the heat pours down, and they wear less and less clothing, just the fugitive touch of one man's hand on her arm is pregnant with meaning for all parties. The lazy contentment of the early days has given way to something deeper, more anxious.

One day a tropical storm arrives: All three of them taking refuge in an empty building that could pass as a beach house, if it had anything other a stone floor and carved-out holes for windows. They wait on the floor for the storm to pass, the local man lingering on a cigarette, the woman resting her head on the first man's shoulder. *Are you planning to stay a while?* the second man asks. This subject has never been broached before; previously, each day had tumbled into the next, with not a thought of consequence. The woman knows what the man is really asking: *Are you planning to stay here with me?* The dreaded moment has arrived. She immediately climbs up, out of range of both of the men, and sighs. *I'm not sure,* she says.

That was the worst thing she could say, because from then on, she is out of the conversation. As if sapped of all energy, like reptiles, they lie in the sun, afraid to do anything except exist. A few nights later, the two men spend time alone on the beach. She observes them as they gesticulate and hang their shoulders and throw up their hands, and it is clear that things are not taking a happy turn.

Then comes a day which could be empirically described as perfect, the sun so dominant in the sky that one cannot see colors above, only light. The two men swim out towards a floating platform anchored in the ocean, a good half-mile away from shore. Back on the beach, she sits, and waits. As they swim further and further away from her, their tiny arms grow nearly comical in their quick little movements. It is actually a relief to be by herself, swarmed with only her own thoughts. Perhaps if she invented a new story— something to keep them all together a little longer. But it is too hot, too beautiful, too everything to even think.

The girl from the convenience store is also on the beach, her limbs all pale and slathered with suntan oil, and the two of them get to talking. *You still have money?* the girl asks, and the woman, reenergized with some of her former bluster, says, *Oh yeah, of course. What should we buy next? Beach balls, maybe? A whole beach full of beach balls?*

When are you leaving? the girl asks.

What? The woman laughs harshly. *Do you want me to leave?*

No, says the girl. *I just thought you had a home to go back to. Or are you staying here for good?*

That's it. She has arrived at a new plot. *Let me tell you,* she says. *It's a long story—*

And someone screams *Help!* A few random fingers point towards the sea, towards the direction of the floating platform. The woman scrambles to her feet, hand shielding her eyes, squinting for a look. There is a flurry out in the ocean, waves crashing on waves, a sudden storm without dark skies or rain. She watches the floating platform where the two men had been a few seconds before; it is now rocking, bobbing, empty.

Unaware she is holding her breath, she watches.

Someone is swimming away from the platform, towards the beach. Just one pair of arms, one bobbing head as big as an insect's. Still nothing on the platform, no other human movement in the waves. She watches as the convenience store girl, suddenly in command, calls together some of the other locals on the beach. A motorboat's engine splutters to life, and the vessel hops into action, banging against the tide as it heads out towards the lone swimmer. Still only the one pair of arms, the one bobbing head, the lone swimmer agonizingly slow in his progress as he makes for the beach.

She watches as boat and man meet, only a few hundred yards from shore. The man is pulled aboard, and the boat cuts a sharp turn back towards the beach. Her phone decides to ring at that moment. As always, she refuses to answer it, and it is still ringing when the boat draws close enough for her to see the face of the man. It is the local man, gasping for air, somehow staring right at her.

Next day, late afternoon: The woman is packed, sitting alone in the town tea shop, ready to return to whence she came. The first man's body has yet to be recovered, but the explanation seems simple enough: *The riptides around here can be brutal,* says the man who owns the tea shop. He offers her another kettle of *pu erh* tea (good for the digestion). She can only nod at his words; she nods at everything now.

The second man enters the shop, and without asking for permission or making any sort of attempt at pleasantry, he sits with her. *It happened so fast,* he says. *One second he was there, the next he was gone. I couldn't find him. It was all I could do to swim back.*

She nods.

You believe me, don't you? he says.

She nods again.

Do you think—the local man starts, then catches

himself. *If you're ever in the area again...*

She nods. Everyone is too polite to shatter the illusion.

They make their goodbyes at the local train station. For a moment the local man and the woman exchange a look, as if to say: *Is it time to tell the truth yet?* No, there is one last final exchanged look between them. Something too sad to be a smile, too contemplative to be truly disconsolate. No truth, not here ever. No need for it.

And the man walks off down the road, his thumb stuck out to hitch a ride, afflicted with a fresh limp, as if he has inherited the condition from the first man. On the train, the woman looks through the photos she has taken, all of them from her first few days in town; they all look alien, unnatural. She comes across a final photo she took of the beach, before she met either of the two men: in the shot, the beach is empty, the palm trees lolling, the sea frozen just beyond. She closes her eyes and sees the three of them under the trees, their backs to the person taking the photo, eternally unknowable, looking out to sea, which is now rolling, cresting.

Story 3: Early Spring

A song for ghosts.

If the first story takes place at all hours, and the second story takes place mostly in the light, concluding at sunset, then this story is nocturnal in nature. Sounds are diminished, or given fearful volume at certain moments, and the town has a lonely air to it that compels one to seek the company of others in warm little noodle shops, or surrender completely and wander off into the fog, never to return.

Autumn lingers, fog general everywhere. It is early evening, and a man (male actor #1) has arrived in town, alone. He is clearly a world traveler, in plain T-shirt and

jeans, carrying a beat-up acoustic with him, no plans
or reservations past the next few minutes. He has been
sharpened by his travels like a blade, with all thoughts
whittled down to practicality: find food, sleep, useful
camaraderie. Within minutes he is inside the noodle shop,
regaling the owner and her customers with a few songs,
happy to appear boisterous and silly and *different*, the
foreign traveler exploiting his foreignness. At the end of
his performance he admits he has no money to pay for his
noodles, but would be happy to sing a few more songs and
entertain the customers if that will suffice.

For the old woman that runs the noodle shop, that
will not suffice. Off to the kitchen with him, and make
sure those dishes are spotless! Taken aback but taking it
all in his stride (because travel is all about managing
disappointments, in the end, and besides, if he works hard
enough, maybe he can bum a room off this old bird for the
evening), he settles in at his temporary gig as the customers
leave and the shop shuts down for the night. He has been
composing a song—he has a few chords down, a few stabs
of whistled melody that may stick, but nothing in the way
of lyrics—and it catches the attention of the old woman,
who used to be a folk singer back in her day. *You remind
me of my old husband,* she says. *Good for nothing but singing
and having a good time.*

And what else is there? the man replies, and they both
laugh.

The woman doesn't have many memories of past
days—*You get to a point where you start forgetting more than
you remember,* she sighs—but her recollection of music
is good. They find common ground on a particular song
and both sing it, not with gusto or bravado, but the way
you might sing something at the end of a long day, where

the breaths between lines are just as important as the lines themselves, and it feels good to get something out without taxing yourself.

And then both the man and the old woman, as if sensing it simultaneously, turn to look at the front of the shop. Pressed up against the window is a young woman (lead actress), looking disheveled and lost, her eyes pleading, her hand held up against the glass as if trying to push her way through.

The man and the old woman immediately let her in, and sit her down for noodles and tea. She is shivering, small and disoriented, yet she is gaining a certain calm, as if she knows what she must do. She is from somewhere else, and it has been a few years since she has been to this town. Some things have changed, and it is difficult to find one's way in the fog.

The old woman throws together a bowl of noodles as a lifeline, and the woman accepts gratefully. *I heard the music*, she says. *One of our favorite songs.*

You and who else? he asks.

My boyfriend. From back in the revolutionary days. Not so long ago, but not so close that it is fresh in everyone's heads. Slowly at first, but with gathering strength, she tells a tale: her boyfriend was an activist, and not one of those quiet ones. One of those college idealists, packed in a classroom late at night with like-minded people, drinking and arguing and pontificating and laughing, because we were innocent enough to laugh about such things back then. He didn't want to leave the city, but he knew he would be arrested eventually, so he came out here to hide with some friends. *I came out to be with him on the weekends, when I could, when I wouldn't be missed.*

We see episodes of her with her boyfriend (male actor

#2): we always see them rooted in a particular location, as if they are physically a part of the town, inseparable from it. Lying on the beach, her head on his chest, picking at something on his arm. Sitting at an outdoor café, watching life move around them, lost in their individual thoughts. At the temple deep in the bamboo forest, near nightfall, candles lit up around them, bundled up close together against the darkening day. Watching an oldie at the local cinema, both of them caught up in laughter. In the noodle shop, deep in animated conversation about something, oblivious to the immediate world.

Is that tea store still open here? she asks. *We used to get tea there often. "Early Spring," that's what they called the local black tea. My boyfriend loved it, he said if he ever got in on the ground floor of the new government, the first law he'd pass would be to make Early Spring the national drink. Started calling me Early Spring just for fun. Now I sit here years later, and no one remembers him, and no one outside this town drinks Early Spring.*

A final image of happiness: the man trotting over with a bicycle that has seen shinier days, the two of them riding the winding mountain road into the bamboo forest, he mashing the pedals furiously, she riding side-saddle and eventually getting off to help push him forward, up the hill.

What happened to him? the traveling musician asks.

The police finally found him. I was with him when it happened. He didn't put up a fight—no, all he wanted to do was debate with them! Like maybe he could change their political views if he kept at it long enough. They took him away in a car... and...

A bad twist of fate: a wrong turn on one of those mountain roads, the car plunging off the side. Everyone aboard dead.

Maybe it was better that way. What if they made it all the way back to the city? Maybe he'd be getting out of prison now but he would be lost, behind the times, no place in this new world. She sighs. *So now I'm back, years later, and I'm the same way. I don't recognize this town anymore. Don't recognize anything anymore. Sorry to trouble you—*

She stands to leave, but the musician says *Wait.* He proposes they walk around the town together, if she's up for it; he doesn't have a place to spend the night anyway, and maybe if they stroll for a bit, some of the memories will come back to her. She agrees, and they head into the misty night, visiting the places of memory: the movie house, the outdoor café, the beach. On his part, the musician is caught between solicitousness, desire and curiosity, and can only drift slightly behind her as she walks, mute. Flickers of recognition cloud her eyes, as if intellectually she remembers these places, but the emotional connection has been lost. She is sorry she has wasted the musician's time.

It's funny, she smiles weakly. *I thought coming here might bring him back, somehow. It was a stupid fantasy.*

Wait, the musician says again. They are on the road near the beach, and just beyond them are those familiar palm trees facing the sea. He admits that he wasn't around for those days of revolution—he was too busy traveling around the world, and he doesn't know much except maps and music. But at least there's music. He starts strumming a song, something that dates back to those old days, a simple pop song, something that might be silly to some ears, and yet he throws himself into it, and for the first time, a laugh escapes her. *Thanks for taking me back*, she says.

Something is coming out of the fog towards them— something squat and wide, like a creature with a giant lower half. Both of them caught up in the atmosphere of the moment, they grab each other like scared teenagers, rooted to the spot. It is not a creature; as it draws nearer, it is clear that it is a man with a bicycle. It is the boyfriend, dressed in the same clothes he had in that long-ago summer, with the same burning, almost cocky smile he had when he was discussing politics.

Finally found you, he says. *Want to go?*

Wait, the musician says, for the third and final time. *This is impossible—*

You can see him, right? I can see him too, she says. *It's a fantasy. Like I said.*

She embraces the musician, silencing his opposition, and joins her boyfriend on the bicycle. They begin pedaling away, down onto the beach, parallel with the shoreline. The musician walks after them, then breaks into a jog, and then a blundering run as he tries to keep up with them, but the bicycle gets farther and farther away, until it disappears into the dark and mist. Doggedly, the musician keeps running, following the tracks left by the bicycle, and then the tracks disappear into nothing in the sand. He stares at the dead end for a moment before the waves sweep in and erase more of the tracks. He looks towards the ocean, down the beach, for any evidence of anything, and sees nothing.

Back at the noodle shop, the old woman and the tea shop manager are enjoying some fresh-brewed oolong, having a laugh, as the musician enters. *Where you been at?* the old woman says in that lovely gruff tone of hers. *You haven't finished the dishes yet.*

Hey young man, the tea shop manager offers a cup. *Have some Early Spring.*

Sorry, the musician says. *The woman needed some help.*

What woman? the old woman asks.

The one who was here earlier. The one from revolutionary

days, who told us about the boyfriend who died.

Is that so? The old woman looks honestly puzzled. *I don't remember anyone being here. But I forget things faster than I can remember them these days...*

Wait a sec, boyfriend who died? the tea shop manager says. *Back in revolutionary days? What was the girl's name?*

She didn't say—but she said her boyfriend named her Early Spring as a joke...

No way. Impossible, the manager says, but behind his conviction is a bit of fear. *I remember them. They came to my shop all the time. Made that Early Spring crack. But they're both dead. Police came and got both of them, they both died in a car accident. You remember, Granny?*

I told you, I don't remember...

She was here, the musician insists. *Come on Old Woman, you made noodles for her.*

I remember I made noodles for you, the old woman snaps, irritable, *and you still have to pay me for them.*

She was here! Incensed and confused, the musician storms out of the shop, leaving the tea shop manager to stare at the old woman, the question in his eyes.

He was playing an old song, the old woman says. *Old music brings up a lot of stuff.*

Outside the tea shop, on the street, the young musician stands helpless, looking all around him at a misty wonderland that betrays nothing. Somewhere far away, he can hear cars, motorcycles, and even the crash of the waves on the beach. He wanders out towards the sea, strumming a song on his guitar to ease his loneliness, and the townspeople trail him, either pulled by the song, concerned for his well-being, or obeying some more ancient prerogatives. Soon they are all assembled on the beach, and he sits cross-legged, his guitar on his lap. Something in him is shaken; his old certainty about things will not return. Raw and open, he begins playing the chords to the song he was improvising earlier, only this time he is not singing, he is playing a song for ghosts, something that requires no words.

CHARGE

TWO PEOPLE ARE IN A SUBWAY CAR: ONE SITting, the other standing with a bicycle. Both of them are a few feet apart, but obscured from the other by rush hour crowds. The one with the bicycle walks it towards the door, anticipating the next stop, hands squeezing at the brakes out of habit. The seated one is poring through the remains of a newspaper left by a previous passenger. The train supplies all dialogue: *thrum-thrums, click-clacks.*

The bicyclist passes and something hits the seated person in the shins. Maybe a pedal, maybe the kickstand, maybe the edge of a gear in the back. The seated person, lost in the fog of thought, reacts in slow motion. What? Pain. Sharp, insistent. Source? Bicycle. Heard before seen: the fragile little whir of the back tire, followed by a cracked shard of ruby where there was once a whole back reflector.

The moment drags on. Bicycle and bicyclist are receding. Time going, going. No acknowledgment of what just happened.

Thank you, the seated one says.

The bicyclist half-turns without stopping, as momentum rules the day. *Fuck you!* the bicyclist hisses. *Get the fuck out of my way!* The train judders to a stop, the doors bounce open, and bicycle and bicyclist are gone.

* * *

    Thank you.

    Respond? Stay quiet? Say it. Those were his thoughts in order, so he says it. He imparts just a touch of lightness to the words, or he likes to think so. Intention is his, reception is out of his control. Anyway, he wants to leave open the possibility that he's half-serious. Best to protect yourself that way. It's a world of overreaction. Better in the old days when there were knives and not guns. Knives require work, a bit of effort. There was a story in the paper about China. Man walks into a kindergarten, stabs 20 kids. Sure some of them died, but most survived. Better odds than you'd get over here.

    It's his mother. He's never been in therapy, fuck therapy, but it's his mother. She's infected him with this obsession over mortality. One ailment after another, what was she on about now? Four doctors in the last year, because no one could stand her for long:. Five life-threatening diseases during the same period. He couldn't avoid her. No matter where he was, she had a knack for finding him. Once he took a week in Paris without warning, just to be away, and somehow she figured it out and called the U.S. embassy to track him down. He was on a bike trek with a group of Americans, and they were just about to enter the *Musee D'Orangerie* (Napoleon and the Godfather, they loved their oranges), home of Monet's Water Lilies, when their friendly guide from New Zealand answered his phone and then handed it to him. *Hey man, they say it's your mother and it's an emergency.* The tourist family from Ohio alongside him gave him such warm looks of concern that he couldn't bear to tell them that it was just Mother dying for the umpteenth time from something-or-other. *Mom,* he would say into the phone to hold her up, *Mom, Mom, Mom,* and it was no use, she just would not stop talking, and why did he go off on a trip without telling her? If he hung up she would call him right back and keep right on going as if no time had passed, no interruption had taken place. And eventually he had stopped hanging up at all, for he had come to worry that this could be that one critical phone call, like someone saying *bomb* on an airplane, and yes, this time it really was a bomb.

His girlfriend had stopped asking him about Mother. She would get calls sometimes too. He'd be three blocks away buying groceries, his phone on vibrate and ignored. One missed call would do it. His girlfriend's phone would buzz, she would say in her politest voice, *Hi, Mrs.*—and Mother would say, dead as an assassin, *Get him on now.* His girlfriend used to ask, *What's up with her?* In a very reasonable tone too (see, it's all about modulation). He was dying to talk about it, but he knew that once he started it would never stop, there would be years of it, and it would be way more than she could be expected to handle and she would leave. So he would say nothing. The energy expended in holding it all back would leave him sullen, and pretty soon Mother was a topic to be completely avoided.

His girlfriend had other priorities anyway. She was working out of the apartment. This was big, this thing she was working on. *Redefining the paradigm,* she had said, and she had gotten it into her head that it might make a superb name for a company. *RePar* or something like that. She had tried explaining the concept to him once: at the beginning of the day, think of a word to characterize your dream at that given moment. (*Dishwater*, he immediately responded. *You have to be serious for this to work*, she frowned.) Enter that word on the website, and immediately you are connected with others who have entered that same word that same day. Imagine all of you, imbued with the same passion and same purpose around the same concept, hooked into a giant chat room, or a giant video conference. Conversing, sharing ideas, sum greater than the parts. Active discussion, active learning. Think of the educational applications, the collaborative projects. He had thought about it, and then she said it would take about $10 million to get it off the ground. The guys from Google were interested, but she had said no. Their interest was in the database, the marketing potential. She was determined that this thing would remain pure. So she was on the couch all day, making phone calls, charged with enthusiasm and goodwill and good cheer. It really was a beautiful thing to watch. It would make him feel guilty that he was the only one to witness it. Then he would remind himself that they were still together only because it was the only way they could afford to live in this downtown San Francisco apartment. (Or at least he suspected that was the only reason she was still around.)

The word *source* is the root of the problem. She considers it a verb, he said no way. He knows it is hopelessly out of touch to think like this, he knows he is nothing more than a weed buckling in the wind of tech progress, but he can't help it. Hours have been wasted on the debate over *source*. The irreconcilable gap has been established.

Paid parking is the root of the problem. One rotten hot September day they decided to drive down to Big Basin for the 11-mile loop hike. She was all *great, let's go go go*, before she found out that day parking there was eight dollars. Add it to the gas costs and it just wouldn't fit their budget. Better to go by bus. We can take a few buses and then hike up to the park. It would take four hours to get there, compared to ninety minutes by car. *Look, I'll pay for the parking*, he said. *Why is this such a big deal?* They ended up not going. It just didn't make sense to him. It's getting to the point where not much about her is making sense to him. She wears the same flip-flops she had when they met four years ago, and at this point whole chunks of them are gone, as if a great white shark gnawed them off. He worries that she will always be this way.

The homeless guy outside their front door is the root of the problem. Usually he camps a few streets down, close to the YMCA, except when it rains (quite often these days), and then he comes to their place, because they have a nice wide awning. He has some nice bedding and a bunch of take-out boxes from the local Chinatown restaurants that take pity on him, and in the morning there will be chicken bones, tattered aluminum foil and a puddle of piss. During the night, the homeless man coughs. Never continuously, not very loudly, but always at the most inopportune time, just as he's struggling to sleep one floor above. It's like the homeless man knows his biorhythms to the second and is taunting him. He tried talking to the man once, asking him to leave, and all he got was garbled swear words and spittle that landed right on his nose. He immediately ran into the house and washed his face. His girlfriend is understanding. She brings the homeless man leftovers sometimes. She decries the politicians who are sweeping these people under the rug. She has heard stories of homeless people getting apprehended and bused down to San Diego, where they would stay and never dirty San Francisco's neighborhoods again. He imagines a Cold War between cities, homeless people getting bused back and forth like battalions. He smells the man's piss, even when he's miles away. He imagines taking a baseball bat to the man's head. The only question would be the getaway, especially if the man made noise as he finished him. One time he told his girlfriend his intention. She gave a horrid little laugh, patted his arm. *You wouldn't have it in you,* she told him. She is right and he hates that she is right, and he also hates himself for having these thoughts. Contradiction, heal thyself.

They rarely see each other. During the day while she's at home he's a driver for hire, crowd-sourced, 35 dollars an hour, gas expenses his, and somehow he always ends up with a fare that takes him all the way to San Jose, where he idles for hours, hoping someone else in the area pings him for a ride so the trip down will be financially worthwhile. In the evenings he drags himself back home, the skin between his eyebrows twitching from the stress of dealing with pedestrians who are drunk or high or insane or worse. She is usually out at another networking happy hour known only to those who are plugged in. His phone pings, and it is a fare or it is Mother, or both simultaneous, or even worse, he is with a fare and Mother calls, and he never looks in the rear view mirror because he can imagine what is going through the head of his fare as he says, *Mom, Mom, Mom.* The street lights even work against him as they stick themselves to red and he sits there, Mother's voice an ongoing rasp, his shoulders bunching up around his head, the passenger in back clearing his or her throat, nothing moving.

* * *

This is her fourth bicycle. She can't avoid that fact. When she sees the bicycle in the garage it's not just a bicycle, it's not just her bicycle, it's her fourth bicycle. Her husband reminds her. He especially reminds her of the third bicycle, because she left it out in the street, unlocked, for literally five minutes—okay, maybe six or seven, because she had forgotten something in the house and had to run in to find it. Her pad and pen, come to think of it. Still clinging to the hope of becoming a writer. She writes pages and pages of notes to herself, usually just phrases, flotsam from the day, maybe a line of clever dialogue. If she is lucky she will stumble on these scribbles a few years later, and the first (and sometimes only) thing that will register is how much her handwriting has changed. Anyway, that day it had taken her six or seven minutes to find her pad, and by the time she was back out the front door her third bicycle was gone. So this is the fourth.

Her husband focuses on things like that. A very focused man, about certain things. Things and things and things. Frequent flyer miles are important. He has a specific credit card for the miles, and Black Friday and Cyber Monday are the big days, game-planned for. Coupon websites, group deals. Purchase, note, reconfirm miles on statement. He knows how to spend to save. In a better life he would be one of those financial advisors on the cable news network, sticking his chin out whenever he gave a particularly strong tip. When he gets a notice from the tax board claiming he owes another seven hundred dollars he fights it all the way. It takes years, and even if a resolution is reached it never seems to end, because by that time another tax bill has been sent. *Why not just pay and be done with it*, she says, and he says with that forbearing, theatrical smile of his, *It's the principle of it.*

Lately he has been all about their wills. Everything must be in order, because he has seen what happens when things aren't spelled out. At his office every day, suited up, sitting in conferences, legalizing with potential clients and foes, he sees what happens. This sort of thing isn't her. She never looks at things like trusts and contingencies and legacies. Sure someday she might be a vegetable in a coma ward and no one will know what to do for lack of instructions. Doesn't matter, she wouldn't be in a position to care anyway. She knows it's bad, it's reckless. Why leave any iota of doubt when it can be taken advantage of by another? Yet she likes that thrill, that little twinge of excitement that comes from leaving herself open.

His latest thing is marathon running. Okay, no issue with that, a hot healthy body at home is good, even if he's usually too tired from his workouts to actually do anything once he gets home. But the running is a sore subject. Years ago she recommended Murakami's *What I Talk About When I Talk About Running* because she loves Murakami, or rather she loved Murakami. This was back in the days when she hoped that he would love what she loved. He ignored the recommendation back then, and then years later when he got serious about this running thing he came across the book on his own, fell in love with it, and asked her why didn't she ever recommend this fantastic book before. She reminded him, he forgot that she reminded him, and from that point forth he was obsessed with Murakami. Just the way he would recite some of the lines from that book— *Pain is inevitable. Suffering is optional*—made her look at it in a different light, and not a good one. Or how about: *I've always done whatever I felt like doing in life. People may try to stop me, and convince me I'm wrong, but I won't change.* God, how fucking entitled that sounded, out of context! Her husband had moved on from there to Murakami's other books. She didn't hear the end of it. *That cucumber stuff in* Norwegian Wood *is so odd, but I love it...* She had dropped

Murakami after he went from first-person to third-person in his later novels, and now her husband has been haunting her with her own reading past. The other week she bought a used book at Green Apple and on the first page, in very pretty handwriting, were the words *My darling: I want to share with you my favorite author. What's mine should be yours.* Originally it said *What's mine is yours* but the *is* had been crossed off.

That is her husband's way though. Sink teeth into something, refuse to let go. Always at his best with a solitary goal to wrap his OCD around. Once he starts talking about something he will keep on going. The trouble is, his stories lack a point. He'll be at dinner with family or friends, recounting something that happened at the office earlier in the day. The telling is comprehensive, exact and without any kind of narrative grace. One thing after another, everything thudding at the same undifferentiated speed, the same tone. He doesn't realize that what he's talking about contains minutiae particular to his job, beyond the grasp of any normal, sane, regular person. You don't realize there is a punch line until after it's arrived and he punctuates with a gasping *ha-ha-ha.* What to do then? Smile. Switch the subject. His family doesn't even pretend to listen anymore. Vacant eyes, rictus grins, and just as his story goes opaque, they immediately turn their attention to something else, someone else. The first time she witnessed his family do that to him it was over dinner. Straight up ignored his words. In the middle of one of his sentences someone asked something completely unrelated of someone else, and everyone jumped in and over him. She flinched. He kept on talking, and talking. He just didn't get it. That circuit in his head to pick up on social cues had burned out, or never existed.

Now he's in trouble at the office. He does his job well, in a mechanical way. The technical judges would give him a 9.8. But he is fixated on being correct, not diplomatic. She hates office politics too. But what can you do? He should have made senior partner by now but he's ticked too many people off. He is completely unaware of his effect. You point out something someone did wrong, it's the person who ends up offended, not the thing. The thing, the thing, the thing. If nothing else, no one wants to talk to him because once he starts, well, you know. She has pointed this out to him, in subtle and obvious ways. He nods and he averts his eyes and he says he understands. Doesn't matter.

He's thinking about changing law firms. *Well, great, quit*, she thinks. What is that, five jobs in seven years? Magic seven. Seven-year itch. Somehow they have gone from Albany to DC to Los Angeles to San Francisco. More expensive each time. Pretty impressive. You quit a job once or twice, okay, it wasn't a good fit. Five times? Look in the mirror. She has said as much to him.

She knows she's fucked up too. Got into a print publishing career in the middle of the dot-com boom. She can do a galley like no one's business. Great. To get work she's had to learn technical writing. Right now she's working on a camera instruction manual. She's fixated on those cute little graphics at the front of the book. The camera has eyes, a button nose, a squiggle for a mouth. In one panel the edge of the camera's head is cracked open from getting dropped on the pavement. Its eyes are shut, its mouth is wide open with pain. In another the camera is scrunched with distress under exposure to the sun, its pipe-stick arms wiping the sweat with a handkerchief. She gets emotional every time she sees these graphics. Upset. They remind her of being a kid and being vulnerable and feeling just everything at once. The manual is taking much longer to complete than it should due to random moments like this. She should work harder, emphasize quantity over quality because that's where we all are right now, but things like this trip her up. Her husband never judges or mentions it. He just smiles and cuddles and talks about his day, and even she treats it as white noise at this point, but it's comforting.

Today she's bringing his cell phone to him at the office. They're refurbishing offices at the firm and somehow he's been shunted into the one needing the most work. (Just plain disrespect at this point, she thinks.) Only one power outlet working, so no place to charge his phone. Can't they provide a power strip? *Sure, I can put in a request, but they're just so inefficient at the office,* he says. So he charges at home. Actually she charges for him because he always misplaces the phone. She has a knack for finding it. It's her one indisputable contribution to the marriage. She doesn't mind, usually, because he does stuff for her, like clean the gunk out from under her toenails. He enjoys it, and she does too. Both in bed, she'll watch the TV and he'll be lounging at a right angle to her, cleaning her up. Better than a massage, maybe better than sex.

Today, though? Today she's kind of pissed, because he forgot his phone, like he often does, and she is in a mood where she would prefer to stay inside, and think, and maybe cry a bit. Hormones, most would say upon a glance. Her husband never says that. She believes she does rather well overall. If an argument ever threatens to get heated, he will simply turn away and lose himself in his thoughts. Most women would prefer to keep talking and ranting ad infinitum. Most women would trail behind as their husbands moved from room to room, refusing to let it go. But she gives him space and gives herself her own space. She's rather proud of herself for that. Today, though: it's not a day for understanding. Why doesn't he have his phone with him at work anyway? Doesn't he need it for what he does? He probably ends up using someone else's phone, or a secretary's phone. Peccadilloes, that's the word. She likes that word.

Today, though: No. Mainly because she was throwing up this morning, and she suspects something. She must get to a drug store and buy that kit. She wills herself not to think about that right now. She really hates her fourth bicycle. It's a big, tank-like thing, which seemed like a good idea when she bought it. Now she realizes her error every time she has to drag it up the stairs from the curb, or tries to chain the thick top tube around an equally thick telephone pole and the u-lock doesn't quite reach all the way around. The gears are malfunctioning too. Every time she puts it in sixth or seventh (naturally, the gears she uses most), the bike seizes up and grinds every few hundred feet. It's easily the most disliked bicycle she's ever had. Of course it's never come close to getting stolen, and of course she's owned it longer than any of her other bicycles. She's tempted to leave it outside her building, unlocked, for say, six or seven hours. Maybe that would do it.

The train is stopping. She has to get out. Damn phone in her hands, almost slipping free. Why didn't she put it in her backpack? Move, move now before it's too late and you get halted short of the closing doors. Grab the bike firmly. Compensate for shifting momentum as the train jerks to a stop. As if throwing herself off a cliff, she makes her move.

* * *

When the train doors slide open to let him in a few

minutes before, the words *Mind the platform gap* rang in his head. He didn't think too hard about why that phrase had popped in there. He read once about car crash victims who were already dead when police arrived, and yet they would still be speaking, the last thought going through their minds getting repeated over and over. *I want my mommy, I want my mommy, I want my mommy.* Marionettes on a tape loop. *Mind the platform gap* was the same way.

When he unfolds the stray newspaper on his seat and sees a Hong Kong dateline, it comes back to him. Spoken in a clipped, half-British accent on the Hong Kong subway's PA. *Please mind the platform gap.* Kind of jowly, the way the vowels would just hang there. It wasn't sexy, but there was something enticing about it. This was back when he traveled. He was discovering stuff back then. In Hong Kong a decade ago, they still had CD stores. He could find jazz imports and bootleg concerts for bands like Roxy Music and Crowded House. That in turn reminds him of a copy of an old letter he found the other day. He had typed it to a girl he knew in college. They were both on summer break; she was tending bar in some ritzy getaway up in the Hamptons, and he was at his family's home down in Virginia, down with the trees and the heat and the rain. It was back when his father was still alive and absorbing most of Mother's blows. The letter he had written was in response to a letter she had written to him—who knew where it was now. At one point in the letter he had written, *Before I go any further, I have to say that you have an interesting conversational style in your letter writing.* Jesus. What the fuck. Later on in the same letter he wrote: *If I have a major weakness in life, it's CDs. If anyone ever wanted to rob me, they shouldn't take the stereo or computer, hell, grab all the CDs.* That was even more embarrassing. How empty and soulless it sounded now.

Nothing ever happened between him and that college girl. She ended up with the Rhodes Scholar guy and who knew if they were still together or where she was now. That was the way it went in college, a lot of women, a lot of letters, a lot of nothing eventually happening. Infatuation was free back then. Later it became much more expensive, like his trip to Hong Kong. There was that Japanese woman he met in grad school, a friend of a friend, and she mentioned that she would be in Hong Kong for the holidays. *Hey, me too,* he said, even though he didn't know he would be traveling to Hong Kong until that very moment. He spoke to her on the phone a few times before the trip, long distance. He put it on his parents' phone card and later he found out they were charged $400 for his calls. Mother loved that one. He found out she was from Kobe, where they have their own regional dialect, and he learned how to say *How goes it: Nani shiton ja?* So when he finally saw her again, a thousand dollars and a few thousand miles later, just before New Year in the Kowloon Tong train station, he said to her, *Nani shiton ja?* She gave a brief laugh, not a bad reaction but not as demonstrative as maybe he would have expected or liked. He should have taken it as a sign.

They stayed in a cramped hotel near Mongkok, where the bathroom floor is the shower floor and the shower has to be heated for a few minutes before using. They had their own beds (standard room layout) and there was no place to pile their backpacks except between them. She had a very dignified way of sleeping that impressed him. Her hands would be crossed over her stomach, she would breathe very gently, and her cheekbones got very stark. He doesn't remember much else from that time. He was into anime music then and always got a kick over how they mangled the lyrics whenever they were in English. He fondly recited some from his favorite song to her: *Things you always do is only for you, it's not changed since we started in this place… I know you're staying, you know I'm going, keep two hearts one, anytime whoa whoa…* (He warbled a good *whoa*, it was enough to get a laugh.) *You see your future, I see my dreaming, there's no good-bye even being all alone…* She had a habit of squinting with her left eye, while her other would grow disproportionately larger of its own accord. It was like she was forever half-skeptical, half-awestruck. It was hard work to truly delight her, but when one of his jokes landed and he got a full laugh out of her, it was like being on an aircraft carrier, announcing mission accomplished.

Looking back on it, it was destined to never go anywhere. He should have known when she told him she liked that British voice saying *Mind the platform gap.* She always preferred British men. The accent and all that. He almost came out and told her that he was in love with her. She probably sensed it. She said to him once, *I am glad there is no meaning in our relationship.* He knew what she meant to say. He couldn't help taking that statement at literal value though. *Hona mata*, he said to her at the airport when they parted, and she gave him a hug that lasted a while. The following Christmas he sent her a photo of them he had taken in Hong Kong, down at the harbor at night with the skyscrapers and lights, and if he did say so himself, they both looked good. A year or so later he sent her another Christmas card, but he goofed and sent her another copy of that same exact photo. He didn't realize the error until after he had mailed the card out. It didn't matter because he never heard from her again, but to him the mistake was inexcusable. It still feels inexcusable now.

How long has it been since he wrote a letter? How long has it been since he wrote anything? His favorite class college course had been the fiction writing workshop where the grad student teacher showed up the first day with a bottle of tequila in hand. (Everything else in that class could not help but be an anticlimax after that.) Maybe he just needed a pen pal. Were there such things anymore? Yes, it was called social media. Internet Bah Humbug! It was Christmastime. He and his girlfriend had had an argument the day before about *It's a Wonderful Life*. With great certitude he had told her that Mr. Potter was the true hero of the movie. Did he really believe that? Maybe he was just being contrarian. Even he didn't know. Maybe he was trying to get a rise out of her. Somehow he had moved from kid to curmudgeon in a single bound. It would be simpler to surrender to the current ways. Take some business classes, learn *something*, get with the current jargon. He looked like a hipster anyway, without even trying. A shambled-looking guy he had passed on the street the other day had called him that: *You fucking hipster, ruining this town!* Well, there was no denying it. He had a pink mustache on his car. He had entrenched himself while the real people, the artists and fuck-ups and folks without resources, had been forced out.

He has been staring at the newspaper without reading it. Last night, a few hours after their Mr. Potter conversation, his girlfriend told him she was dealing with a guy at work. He asked her what she meant by *dealing. He's new on the team. Young. We've got a really good rapport. I don't know. I don't know what it means. I just felt I should be honest and tell you.* He said: *Tell me what? What are you telling me?* She said: *I don't know. That's what I'm telling you.* He said: *What are you thinking?* She said: *It's confusing. It's like I'm not in control of myself.* He said: *Do you want to sleep with him?* She said: *No, it's not that. He's attractive but it's not that.* He said: *Then what?* She said: *It's like wanting to make a connection.*

He said: *What kind of connection?* She said: *I can't describe it.* He said: *What you're not describing is pretty fucking upsetting.* She gave a little shrug of the shoulders similar to what you'd expect from someone who just saw their favorite team lose. She said again: *I just felt I should be honest.* He said: *Should I expect flowers to come for you? Should I expect you to lie about being at an off-site when you're really flying to Hawaii with this guy?* Another shrug. Then his phone rang and they both beat tactical retreats. It was Mother with important news. She had selected a priest to deliver the eulogy at her funeral. When she said the priest's name he ground his teeth. Not *him.* Same guy who delivered the eulogy when Dad died. That time the ceremony had gone as you'd expect any funeral ceremony to go, right down to the ceremonial first heap of dirt on the casket. Everyone half-rose from their lawn chairs to leave, leaving to the rest of it to the grave diggers hired for the occasion, when the priest said in his booming accusatory voice: *Where are you going? The ceremony is not over until the burial is completed.* The priest didn't say another word. No one wanted to be the one to run out while everyone else was stuck, so everyone sat there for the next two hours, watching the two grave diggers, both of them old and clearly past their primes, struggle with their shovels. Finally Mother looked at him, and he rolled up his sleeves and joined in. Two hours of it, and finally it was done, and the priest turned and walked away. Everyone else was too stunned by the whole thing to say a word, so they got in their cars and left. His dad's legacy, the one memory stuck in the heads of everyone who knew him, would be that interminable burial. And he would have to go through it again with Mother. She was being dramatic, telling him about the priest. But the specificity of that physical memory, the sore arms, the raw wood of the shovel handle, somehow convinced him: she was really dying this time.

What he really wants to be is Keith Carradine in *Nashville*. Well, almost. His character is an asshole and a fuck-up in the movie, and yet there's the one scene where he's singing in the bar. He's slept with several women in the audience, and all of them think that song is about them, and hanging in the back is Lily Tomlin, who is married and attracted to him yet has resisted him all through the movie. She knows the song is really for her. You have to forget that Keith sleeps with Lily and then goes on his merry rutting way soon afterwards, while she goes back to her difficult life with uncaring husband and deaf kids. You have to focus on the moment in the song when they both understand each other.

The letter he found the other day to the girl in the Hamptons opens with a Joni Mitchell quote: *They say all romantics meet the same fate someday, cynical and drunk and boring someone in a small café.* That's not bad. He had some taste back then. Now that someday is today, how has he fared? He isn't drunk and he isn't boring someone. He's worse than that. He's insignificant. A bundle of intentions crumpled in a seat.

A bicyclist passes by. Something hits him. Part of the bike. Does he? Dare he? He does. Maybe because the word *intentions* is nagging the insides of his head. The bicyclist is moving away. It doesn't register until after he speaks that the bicyclist is a woman, a ponytail sprouting from the back of her helmet. Would it matter if it were a man? White or black? He likes to think not. He overthinks usually. Not this time.

Thank you.

* * *

She hooks her fourth bicycle around her shoulder and hauls it up the stairs towards the subway exit. Her jaw is like rock. The rail of the bicycles bites into her skin. She likes the pain, it gives extra juice to her fury. Fuck that guy on the subway. Fuck him. Rush hour, I'm just trying to squeeze through, and he gets all fucking *peevish*. She is breathing too hard. She could take the elevator but she can't stand the urine smell. Anyway she must keep moving. She has counted the total number of steps on this stairwell in the past: fifty-nine. An odd number. Odd and too big. She must be around step thirty. Now she is wheezing. She must take it easy. She must take care of herself now.

Her husband is weird around kids. She's seen it with his nephews and nieces. He isn't evil or passive-aggressive or anything like that, and she knows what those things are all about. Her aunt was like that. To her aunt, children were competition. If she wasn't the star of the show, then it had to be made clear to the little upstarts in no uncertain ways. Her aunt's kids were pretty much wrecked by the time they were five. How old were the twins now? Nine? She seriously wondered if they were potty-trained. They hadn't been the last time she had seen them, three years ago. Her husband isn't like that. He definitely is not adept though. Like when her two year-old nephew was climbing up onto a dining room chair with clear designs about getting on the table, and the words just exploded from him: *Justin! No! Get down from there!* It was like he was witnessing a fire. She was certain neighbors down the block must have heard it. Good thing Justin was still too young to be upset by it. Or when Justin tipped over his cup and orange juice spilled everywhere, and he gave this elongated shout. His hands were up by his ears, jiving. Completely out of proportion to the event. Where these dramatics come from, she has no idea. It didn't bode well for him being useful when she had the kid.

(Top of the stairs now: A guy is sitting cross-legged just beyond the fare gates, playing guitar and singing blues. Some of his strings rattle. This is always the hard part, getting past the gates with a bicycle. You have to take the bicycle through the swinging emergency door, park it for a moment, then go back through the door and pay your exit fare. If you're honest. If you have integrity. She is, she does. The guitarist smiles at her. Maybe a leer. He smells of stale sweat. Better than stale urine. Happy holidays.)

Maybe they should move to Singapore. She has heard good things about that place: a real family town. She's had enough of guns and bigotry and taxes and decay. Singapore has gardens that look like they're from the movie *Avatar*. Cheap food everywhere. She likes the heat too. She's a lightweight in that regard. Mark Twain had it right with San Francisco. When they moved out here she said to her husband, we just need two things: A car and central heating. They got the heating but there was nowhere to park. It wasn't safe to drive anyway. This is the first city she's lived in where the pedestrians are crazier than the drivers. Trudging through the crosswalk on a red light, like they were wandering into their bathrooms at five in the morning. Or people in motorized wheelchairs, rocketing down the street, grim and clenched and leaning forward all the time. We get it, you're disabled. Or the guy who insists on jogging during lunch hour downtown, when the streets are at their fullest, and yelling *Out of the way! Move it!* everywhere he goes. She hopes she sees someone like that right now. She will run him over, happily. Give him a little extra to the face with the back tire. Maybe roll back and forth over him. Just like kneading dough.

Moving would be easier if she had gotten that law degree. That's what her dad wanted. *You want to write, that's fine, but get yourself some steady work first and then you can write in your spare time. The way John Grisham did it.* Her husband says it's great she's not a lawyer. Maybe it would all have been simpler, though. If she is going to make a real attempt at writing, she definitely must write something soon. No time once the kid is born. She is prepared for that reality, and has been conservative with her estimates. Eighteen years. What if the child has a mental disability? A lifetime, perhaps. Good thing they've never lived in Marin. For some reason breast cancer is high in Marin. Maybe they can hire a nanny, if they can afford it. *If.* Earlier in the day she found a bunch of writing notes from an unspecified time in the past. Just scabs of words. *Desert days.* By themselves, they could mean anything. A cry from the soul, a New Age album. Or how about this one: *Decidedly sour.* It's like carrying on a conversation with a nutjob. She is furious with herself. She hates the phrase *attention to detail,* it makes her think of job evaluations, and yet it is clear that she lacks it, and it is killing her nonexistent writing career.

Outside the day is cloudless and bright. It's Santa pub crawl day. Folks in Santa suits of all shapes and sizes stream past. About half of them are already drunk. She could use a good fucking drink right now. Got to learn to stop swearing, she thinks. The kid must avoid real life as long as possible, and that includes swear words. Instead of *fuck* how about *fub. Fubbity-fub-fub. No fubbing way.* When she was a kid she used to say *shit-a-maroo* a lot. It sounded too friendly to be a swear, and she liked the way it rolled off her tongue.

Shit-a-maroo, she says out loud. She thinks of that fubber on the train and it all seems ridiculous. She's seized by a giggle, then another. *Shit-a-maroo, shit-a-maroo, shit-a-maroo.* Now the Santas look at her as if she's crazy. *If.* Her husband's flat-iron office building is just a block away and there is much to discuss. Kid, homeless guy, Singapore, a power strip for the cell phone. Her legs have stopped moving. The bicycle squeaks in place. She is having a good little laugh. It's not procrastination, she reassures herself. Procrastination is getting distracted, doing something without purpose. She knows well what she will do, is doing. The Café Royale is having its monthly Beatles karaoke night tonight. She just wants to fub around a little. She will go straight to the café and set herself down at the bar and stare at herself in the mirror, framed by the blood-red drapery against the far wall, and she will sing two, maybe three Beatles songs, depending on how big the crowd is tonight. Everyone will want to sing the old songs like *I Wanna Hold Your Hand* and *And I Love Her*, while she will want to tackle the later songs, like *Bungalow Bill* and *Golden Slumbers*. There will be a clear age gap because most of the people there will either be college kids or Boomers. That is all right. I will be a rare species, she thinks as she starts running, pushing the bicycle ahead of her, attaining speeds she would never reach if she was merely bicycling. She is a bird with crystal plumage.

* * *

Years later he is stepping on board a train during Hong Kong rush hour, and a discreet female voice on the PA advises him: *Please mind the platform gap.* He is on his way to a cheap noodle lunch near Lan Kwai Fong, on one of those impressively smoggy, cloudy days. He hears the words and he jumps back to that time in San Francisco, on the train, the bicyclist running into him, *Fuck you*. The bicyclist probably doesn't even remember at this point, he thinks, as he notes the memory in his journal. I'm the only one keeping this stupid piece of history alive. Still, he smiles, because he realizes how much was different back then: Mother, girlfriend, San Francisco. All of that is gone now, and now here he is, immediately and irrevocably alone, on the other side of the world, and he doesn't mind in the slightest, because he knows that he is in transit. *Mind the platform gap*.

At around the same time she is rubbing her eyes. It's been a long day, her boy is finally tucked in, and she is taking advantage of the quiet to teach herself how to mix music tracks on her computer. She finally has a homemade album finished: simple stuff recorded in the living room, just guitar and vocals, with friends helping out on bass and drums. She will self-publish it and she will never gain fame or note but it will earn her some steady gigs at local wine bars, and she will feel much better about things. She is definitely not going to call the album *Desert Days*. Still, the words *Desert Days* linger in her head. They remind her of the day she was on the train and yelled at that guy. The fourth bicycle. She has chained it to the *no parking* sign in front of her apartment building and left it there. Now as she turns away from the computer she looks out through her window, down on the empty street and the bicycle. In the intervening years thieves have made off with the tires, the gears, the seat. It is just an empty frame lolling against the sign. She has taken great satisfaction from seeing that fubbing vehicle decay before her eyes.

Both of them think of that day on the train, and both

remember what was going through their heads at the conclusion of that day: *We'll probably have to go through the same shit tomorrow.*

ACKNOWLEDGEMENTS

Many thanks to all who have supported and encouraged me, with particular gratitude to Christopher Bernard for his insightful feedback. Mark Weiman of Regent Press for his work in bringing this collection to life, and Sean Miner for the cover design.

Thanks also to the following people who have supported the production of this book:

Sanford Arisumi	Elaine Doyle-Gillespie
Christopher Arnold	Stefan Feist
Doug Bacon	David Grayson
John Bae	Benjamin Greenberg
Stephen L. Bajza	Michael Hansen
James Barber	Marc Hertz
Sean Mclain Brown	Kristina Joie
Erin C.	Celeste Katz
Teresa Chan	Connie Chung Kim
Jackee Chang	Jennifer Lee Kirk
Kris Critchley-Goodier	Terry Howell
Melissa Culross	Scott Hoyt
Ashleigh Emerick	Carrie Kirby

Chris Korhonen
Lynn Landry
Cami Lenett
Sir Jason Lewis, Esq.
Christopher Lin
Howard Lin
Nan Lin
Jon Wai-keung Lowe
Joy Ma
Pawel Malczewski
Doug Meierdiercks
Andrea Mize
Caroline Nevin
Hawlan Ng
Anh Nguyen
Trang Pepito

Sara Perkins
Alex Pico
Mu-ming Poo
Mu Qian
Elizabeth Rho-Ng
Annette Roman
David Saia
Jocelyn Saurini
Mike Schawel
Rahul Shah
Vernon Silver
Ruojie Wang
Tim White (aka Johnny Danglebone)
Henry S. Wright

Finally, a special thank-you to Joanne Chiu—once upon a time, you predicted that we would no longer be friends by the time I had my first published work, and look where we are now.

OTHER *CAVEAT LECTOR* BOOKS

NOVELS

September Snow
by Robert Balmanno

Runes of Iona
by Robert Balmanno

Embers of the Earth
by Robert Balmanno

A Spy in The Ruins
by Christopher Bernard

Voyage to a Phantom City
by Christopher Bernard

POETRY

Chien Lunatique
by Christoper Bernard

CPSIA information can be obtained
at www.ICGtesting.com
Printed in the USA
LVOW11s2358240418
574788LV00001B/60/P

9 781587 903847